THE SASSENACH

THE SASSENACH

Helen B. McKenzie

CANONGATE · KELPIES

First published 1980 by Canongate Publishing Limited
First published in Kelpies 1986

Cover illustration by Jill Downie

Printed in Great Britain
by Cox & Wyman Ltd, Reading, Berkshire

ISBN 0 86241 115 7

*The publisher acknowledges subsidy
of the Scottish Arts Council
towards the publication of this volume.*

CANONGATE PUBLISHING LTD
17 JEFFREY STREET, EDINBURGH EH1 1DR

To the memory of my mother and father
Clare Cameron and Jim McKenzie

CONTENTS

Elspeth's Suspicions are Aroused

Smuggling!

There was a time when that word had conjured up for Elspeth MacLaine the usual romantic picture of rocky coasts, hidden caves and sailing vessels. Now that picture was changing, and so also were Elspeth's ideas of her father's way of life.

"Any day now I could know for certain that I'm a smuggler's daughter!" she mused. "It seems unbelievable!" Yet Elspeth felt a thrill of excitement at such a prospect. "I must have the wild blood of a highland rover in my veins," she said to herself, and her eyes danced with sheer delight at the thought.

Elspeth looked every inch the typical Scots country lass— but by birth she was actually English. In fact, she had never been out of England until 1821, the year before all this happened. Her father had decided to give up his job as a tutor in a boy's school and return to that part of Scotland where he had been born and brought up.

"I'm going back to Glenisla," he had said. "My father has found me a croft in Kilry on the south side of the Glen. I want to be a crofter, tilling the soil and tending my cattle and sheep on the hillside as my people have done for generations before me. Somehow I feel that this is my destiny."

"I can understand your feelings, Sandy," his wife had said. "I'll be happy to go with you to Scotland. Perhaps it will seem like going home for me as well."

In a way that was true. Although she had been born in England and had lived all her life there, Elspeth's mother was also of Scottish ancestry. Both of her great-grandfathers had been Jacobites and had had to flee from Scotland when Prince Charlie's army had been defeated. They had settled in England and their descendants had remained in the South ever since. Those people had never lost their interest in their native land, however, and Elspeth's grandfather had nurtured in her a great love of all things Scottish. The old man had encouraged her to learn about Scottish history, and he was always telling her about the loyalty and the friendliness of the Highlanders.

So it was not surprising that Elspeth had also welcomed the move North.

"In some strange way I feel that's where I really belong too," she had said.

Unfortunately for Elspeth, many of the young people of Kilry didn't prove as friendly as her grandfather had led her to expect. Some of her schoolfellows actually chose to look on her as a foreigner and nicknamed her 'the Sassenach' because of her English tongue. Bitterness towards the English was understandable at that time because of the cruelty suffered by the clanspeople for so many years after the Battle of Culloden. In the case of the school children though, the word 'Sassenach' was probably used on the spur of the moment.

Yet to Elspeth, with her sensitive pride in her Scottish origins, it seemed like total rejection and the continued use of the hated nickname caused her much secret unhappiness.

Life on the croft had at first seemed quite uneventful but gradually Elspeth had become aware that strange happenings were taking place around her. For instance, she had begun to realise that her father and the tenants of neighbouring farms and crofts were often together on secret missions during the long dark nights. She knew that clan forays into neighbouring glens were now a thing of the past, but from what she had read in the history books, together with chance remarks dropped by her elders, she had begun to form the opinion that the men were secretly making highland whisky or *usquebaugh*. This was against the law, but the Highlanders had always had scant respect for laws, and their mountainous glens were well suited to whisky-making and whisky-smuggling.

Elspeth had mentioned the smuggling to no one, but when she was alone, out on the moor herding her father's two cows and their year-old calves, she had been giving the question a lot of thought. As yet she had no idea where the men could be making the whisky, or how they disposed of it, but as she lay in the bracken by the burn one warm July afternoon, she pondered the matter in her mind. Her pet lamb, Daisy, was grazing on the bank, her tail flicking from side to side.

Suddenly, as she lay thinking, Elspeth heard her name being called. She recognised the voice of Rory McNeill, the youngest son of their nearest neighbour. Rory and Elspeth had become good friends, and he never called her the Sassenach – as most of the older boys did – a fact for which Elspeth was grateful.

Before Rory himself appeared at the top of the incline, a sheepdog bounded into view; on seeing Elspeth, it gave a welcoming bark. With ears flattened and tail wagging joyfully, it dashed down the slope, throwing itself upon her and licking her face and hands.

"Down, Ben! Down!" ordered Elspeth, warding him off as best she could, and finally rolling him over amongst the ferns where he lay beside her with tongue lolling out and tail still flapping wildly.

While Elspeth was trying to free herself from the attentions of Ben, Rory arrived, jumping over the whin bushes and slithering down the last few yards to come to a halt beside her. He was a tall, wiry looking boy, his face and limbs browned by exposure to the wind and sun.

"Where did you get Ben, Rory?" asked Elspeth.

"I was up at the house looking for you," said Rory, "and your father was just finished working with the sheep at the *buchts*, so he said I could take him with me. Your mother gave me this *peece* to give you," he added, thrusting out a bulky object wrapped in a cabbage leaf.

"Thank you," said Elspeth, unwrapping the cool green leaf. "Do you want a bit of it, Rory?"

"No, thanks. I've eaten my share, but look at Ben!" he said, laughing. "The way he's watching that scone in your hand you'd think he hadn't seen food for a week, so he'll certainly not refuse a bit. What about doing some guddling then, Elspeth?"

Elspeth, whose mouth was already full, nodded assent, but first of all she seated herself on a boulder and ate the scone and butter her mother had sent, Ben coming in for a generous portion.

Rory, with his sleeves rolled up, was wading in the burn, feeling under the boulders and banks before Elspeth had finished eating, so as she was already barefoot, she tucked up the skirt of her homespun dress and followed him into the water.

Being well practised in the art of guddling, both Elspeth and Rory knew the special hiding places favoured by the trout and were soon shouting with delight as they caught the slithering bodies between their strong brown fingers and deposited them on the grassy bank. Occasionally one or other of them would let a trout slip through their hands but that seldom happened, and by late afternoon they had quite a catch of fair-sized trout to show for their labours.

"We'd better go," said Elspeth at last, noticing the position of the sun. "It must be nearly milking time. I wonder where Maggie and Belle are?" Jumping out of the burn she called to Ben who was standing in the middle of the stream doing his best to catch the trout in his mouth as they flashed past him.

"Oh, Rory, do look at Ben's funny face," Elspeth cried, laughing heartily as the collie raised his dripping beard from the water. But their laughter changed to shrieks as the lively Ben threw himself upon them, giving each in turn a thorough soaking before setting to work to roll himself dry amongst the grass.

Producing a piece of twine from his pocket, Rory now seated himself on the bank of the burn and proceeded to string the trout together while Elspeth ran off to search for her charges, closely followed by Ben and Daisy the lamb.

Fortunately the cattle had only wandered a little farther upstream so Elspeth soon turned them, and then drove them up the slope and on to the moor. The cows themselves knew it was near their milking time, and once they were on the homeward path, they hurried along, with the *stirks* close behind, and Daisy the lamb skipping and dancing at their heels, sometimes leaping in the air and sometimes charging at Ben who was never averse to a bit of fun.

"We're clipping the sheep tomorrow, Elspeth," said Rory. "Will you be coming across?"

"Of course I'll come," replied Elspeth, "but I didn't know you were to be clipping. I thought Father was to start hay-making tomorrow."

"Aye, so he was, but he said he'd put that off till Monday," Rory explained.

"Who else will be at the clipping?" Elspeth asked as they strode along the moorland track, their bare feet covering the rough ground quickly and easily as though they had been wearing strong leather shoes.

"The Farquharsons of Drumedge are coming, and Auld Geordie the shepherd at Mosshaugh. We'll easily manage with them and your father, Elspeth, for we have fewer sheep this year. We lost a lot of ewes with inflammation last winter."

The track they had been following now swung sharply to the left along the hillside and a less well-defined path cut off through the heather to their right. Turning into this path, Elspeth and Rory breasted a slope and came suddenly in sight of the croft that was Elspeth's home. Known as The Shieling, it nestled at the very edge of the moor and consisted of a small cottage with a byre, a stable, and other outhouses attached. Built of whinstone from the moor, and thatched with reeds from the riverside, it had already weathered the blasts of more than a century. Two tall pine trees stood like sentinels above its roof, and its small fields of grass and hay, potatoes, turnips, and ripening grain stretched like a patchwork quilt towards the River Isla. In the rays of the setting sun, the river wound through the valley like a golden ribbon and in the far distance could be seen the pale blue outlines of the Sidlaw Hills.

In front of the house was a square of garden containing vegetables, some fruit bushes, and Sandy MacLaine's collection of beehives. The garden was surrounded by a drystane dyke, and over this dyke, at the very foot of the garden were the sheep pens, familiarly known as *buchts*.

Just as they reached the house Elspeth's mother came out carrying the milking pails. An elegant-looking woman, in spite of her rough homespun clothes, she had the same fair skin as Elspeth. But there the likeness ended, for Mrs MacLaine had vivid blue eyes and straight corn-coloured hair which was drawn tightly back from her face and wound into a thick coil at the nape of her neck. Elspeth's own eyes were grey and her hair, which grew in curly profusion, was deep black.

"I was beginning to wonder if you two had fallen asleep out there on the moor," said Mrs MacLaine, smiling at them. Then, turning to Rory, she said, "I hope you'll stay and have supper with us, Rory. The table is set and we shan't be long."

Rory agreed readily. "Thanks very much, Mrs MacLaine, I'm really hungry." As Elspeth took one of the milking pails from her mother, he followed them into the byre and tied up the cows.

"Look, Mrs MacLaine," he said, with a grin, holding up the string of trout. "Elspeth certainly didn't sleep after Ben and I appeared on the scene!"

"My goodness, no! You have been busy, the pair of you," said Mrs MacLaine appreciatively.

At that moment, Sandy MacLaine's tall broad-shouldered figure appeared in the doorway of the byre.

"By jove, lad, that's a grand catch," he remarked, "where did you get them?"

"Elspeth and I guddled them in the den, Mr MacLaine."

"Well, they're good ones. I'm thinking I'll need to take my rod across to the wee burn myself some evening. But just you come away now and see how our pig is thriving, Rory."

So Rory and Mr MacLaine wandered off to the back of the house where the family's future supply of bacon lay on its side, grunting contentedly in the cool of the evening.

"What a difference I see on that pig!" exclaimed Rory. "If it keeps going like that you'll need to build a new sty for it!" As Mr MacLaine shut in the hens and closed the various outhouses for the night, he and Rory discussed the best feeding for pigs and other farm stock. Then they settled down in the kitchen for a chat while Mrs MacLaine and Elspeth went about the various tasks associated with milking time.

The inside of Elspeth's home was as humble as the outside, and contained only two main rooms – the kitchen-living room to the left of the outside door, and a sort of bedroom-sitting room to the right. Between these two rooms was a small closet, or pantry, which held the various stores and provisions such as the meal *girnel* and the flour barrel. At the far end of this pantry was the milkhouse – a tiny dairy built round with stone shelves to provide a cool resting place for the bowls of milk and cream and the slabs of yellow butter.

The kitchen was typical of most country living rooms of those days. It had whitewashed walls, a stone-flagged floor, and a low, raftered ceiling. Light for this room came from a small window in the front, looking down the Glen, and from a tiny, deep-set window at the side which looked directly on to the moor. A wide, open fireplace held a fire of logs and peat, and a heavy iron kettle always hung suspended over the flame from an iron bar known as the *sway*. Home-cured hams hung from hooks, or cleeks, in the rafters, alongside the oil *cruisies*, which provided a fitful light during the dark evenings. In one corner of the kitchen stood a grandfather clock, and from another corner a ladder ascended to the garret, which was divided into two apartments which served as bedrooms for Elspeth and her parents. These rooms, under the steeply sloping thatch, were each lit by a tiny window under the eaves, and each room contained a built-in bed called a box-bed. Bathrooms were unheard of in those days, and water for all purposes had to be fetched from a spring on the moor.

"Just a minute, Mother!" exclaimed Elspeth as they were about to sit down at the table. "I've forgotten to feed Daisy and the cats."

Elspeth fed her pets, but she didn't take long with her task tonight. She didn't want to miss any of the fun and chatter at the table with Rory. Visitors were few and far between in those isolated homesteads, and Rory was always good company. He knew everyone in the Glen, and invariably had some amusing scraps of gossip to relate. So it was a real pleasure to have him to share their meal of homemade bannocks and cheese, followed by scones with butter and honey, and plenty of warm milk to drink fresh from the cow.

At length Rory rose and pushed back his chair.

"I must be going," he said, "for I'll have to be up early in the morning for the clipping. Thanks very much for the fine supper, Mrs MacLaine. I've enjoyed it."

"You're very welcome, Rory. It's been good for us to have your company," smiled Mrs MacLaine.

"Haste ye back, lad!" said Mr MacLaine. "We're aye pleased to see you. You can tell your father I'll be across to 'Kilwhin' as early as possible in the morning. It has every promise of being a good day so we should get on with the job."

"Rory wants me to go to the clipping too, Mother," said Elspeth as her mother was bidding Rory goodnight at the garden gate.

"Well I've no doubt Mrs McNeill could do with your help in the kitchen, dear, and I'll bake some scones for you to take along. Now don't be going too far over the moor. Remember it will be an early start tomorrow morning," her mother reminded her, as Elspeth and Ben set off to accompany Rory part of the way home.

Returning through the summer evening, Elspeth paused by the sheep *buchts*. Leaning on the dyke she gazed up the Glen to where she could just make out the road to Glenisla and Glenshee. As she gazed she distinctly saw someone at one of the roadside cottages hoist up a line of washing.

Knowing the early-to-bed and early-to-rise habits of the Glen dwellers, this struck Elspeth as being decidedly odd.

"That's queer!" she remarked to herself. "This has been a lovely day. Surely their things should have been dry by now." Then she heard her mother calling to her, so she whistled to Ben and raced him to the gate.

"Do you know what I saw just now, Mother?" she remarked as she washed herself in the kitchen before going to bed.

"No, dear, what did you see?" inquired her mother rather absentmindedly, for she was counting the stitches on her knitting needles.

"I saw someone over on the Glenisla road hanging out a big line of washing! Just imagine, Mother! At this time of night!"

Mrs MacLaine paused in her knitting and glanced quickly towards her husband who was sitting mending his boots in the open doorway of the cottage.

"What was that you said, Elspeth?" her father asked sharply.

Elspeth repeated what she had seen, and, to her amazement, her father laid down his hammer and walked quickly to the foot of the garden.

"Doesn't Father believe me, Mother?" asked Elspeth.

"Yes yes, of course he does. But look at the time, Elspeth," said her mother, pointing to the grandfather clock. "Get away to your bed now, and I'll empty that basin for you. You'll have to be up early in the morning, you know."

Elspeth climbed the ladder to her room, but lying in the darkness of her box-bed she kept wondering why her father could have been so anxious to see the line of washing for himself. As she lay puzzling over this she thought she heard the ring of an iron-shod hoof on the flagstones of the yard and she strained her ears to hear who the late caller might be. No knock came, however, and being tired after her long day in the open air, she soon drifted off to sleep.

Revelations

The sun was streaming in at the tiny attic window when Elspeth woke the next morning, and she could hear the swallows twittering under the eaves.

"Time to get up now, Elspeth," her mother called from the kitchen below. Remembering the sheep clipping, Elspeth rose and dressed herself quickly. The smell of oatmeal porridge boiling in the big iron pot over the fire reached her as she descended the ladder, and the thought of a tasty breakfast of porridge, served with a bowl of rich, creamy milk, made her hurry with her milking chores.

"Mother, who was the visitor that came after I was in bed last night?" Elspeth asked, as she ate her breakfast.

"Visitor, Elspeth? We had no visitor last night."

"Och! You must have dreamt it, Elspeth!" said Mr

MacLaine, entering the kitchen at this point. "Are you not ready yet? It's time we were off."

"Have you fed Daisy?" asked her Mother.

"No, but I'll do that now. Wait for me, Father! I shan't be long."

Having fed Daisy and fetched a bucket of water from the spring, Elspeth pronounced herself ready, and she and her father, with Ben frollicking in front, set off to Kilwhin, Elspeth carrying a basket of scones which her mother had baked for Mrs McNeill.

Before they were halfway over the moor they could hear the bleating of the sheep, the barking of dogs, and the shouting of the men as the flock was driven into the Kilwhin buchts. Rory came to meet them as they turned off the moor into one of the fields and Elspeth and he crossed over to the buchts while Mr MacLaine joined the men where they leaned over the garden dyke discussing the merits of the McNeill vegetables.

It was a beautiful summer morning and a curtain of mist was rolling back from the valley. As Elspeth sat on the top spar of a gate chatting to Rory, the hilltops to the South appeared to rise above the mist like islands out of the sea. Turning to look towards the farmhouse, Elspeth saw a fresh spiral of peat reek rise from the Kilwhin chimney.

"That'll be mother stoking up the fire to boil the kale pot," remarked Rory, grinning, and licking his lips.

"Time I was off to help her then," said Elspeth, and as the men were now discarding their jackets and rolling up their sleeves, she jumped down from her perch and hurried off to the house.

"Come away in, child," called Mrs McNeill in answer to Elspeth's tap on the door. "Rory was just after telling me that you'd be coming to lend me a hand, and it's real glad I am to be having you."

Mrs McNeill was a small, plump, rosy-cheeked Irish woman who still proudly retained her Irish brogue, in spite of many years away from her native land. As Elspeth entered, she turned from her job of cutting vegetables into a big iron pot, like a cauldron, which hung over the fire from the iron sway bar.

"My, that was kind of your mother to send me those scones, Elspeth, and I'm thinkin' I'll be glad of them, to feed those hungry men."

"What shall I do to help you, Mrs McNeill?" asked Elspeth as she tied an apron over her dress.

"You can start to peel the potatoes, Elspeth, and I'll be helping you whenever I've finished with the broth."

So Elspeth spent a busy morning, peeling potatoes, scraping carrots, shelling peas, and doing various other out-door and indoor tasks. Finally, she swept the kitchen floor and proceeded to set the big kitchen table with plates and bowls and cutlery, ready for the meal. She had noticed when the McNeill boys had carried the flagons of drinking water to the buchts, they had also taken the customary jar of whisky for those who might want a stimulant rather than a thirst-quencher. Now she saw that Mrs McNeill had also placed a jar of whisky on the table. Elspeth passed no comment, but she was well aware that the tax on spirits was particularly high at that time, and the inhabitants of the Glen were far from wealthy!

The men were cheerful company as they gathered round the table and one and all enjoyed a hearty meal. When they had finished eating they strolled outside and seated them-selves on a grassy bank nearby. Some covered their faces with their hats and settled down for a nap, but Rory's brother Rab fetched his fiddle and soon they were all tapping their feet to the music and shouting for special request tunes.

"Come away out and hear the music, Elspeth," said Mrs McNeill. So they joined the sheep clippers and even danced a few reels with the more energetic of them.

By the time the clipping had been resumed, one of the Farquharson girls had arrived to lend a hand in the house so Elspeth was free to join Rory at the buchts.

Rory's job was to mark the newly clipped sheep. This was

necessary to prove which sheep belonged to which farm, or croft, each place having its own particular mark. Since the sheep in that little community often grazed together on the moor, the marking process was really essential.

"Look! See that sheep with the funny twisted horn?" asked Rory, pointing to a blackfaced ewe with one horn curved in a peculiar manner.

"I've never seen one quite like that before," said Elspeth, observing it closely.

"That was my pet lamb last year," Rory explained. "I called her 'Crumpie.' She still answers to her name but she's not as friendly as she used to be. Now look across there, Elspeth," he continued, flashing a finger in another direction. "That's my pet the year before last – that big sheep with the white mark on its face."

Elspeth couldn't pick out the right one and Rory had just launched into a more detailed description when his father interrupted.

"Pay attention to your job, now, Rory, and see and mark them well, for there were two or three ewes missing when we gathered them in last night."

"That's not so good news, Tom," remarked Elspeth's father, pausing in his labours.

"They were some of the lot I bought from Ravernie," Mr McNeill explained, "so there's a chance they've made for home again. I'll have to ride up there and see."

"I heard Jock Spence, the shepherd at the Newton, saying he'd lost a few lately," remarked Mr Farquharson. "I just hope we're not in for another spell of sheep stealing."

"I sincerely hope not," rejoined Mr McNeill, "I could ill afford another loss after all the deaths we had through the winter and spring."

The two young Farquharsons, Mr MacLaine, Geordie the shepherd, and one of Rory's brothers were doing the shearing, or clipping. The other boy McNeill was catching the sheep for the clippers, and Mr McNeill himself was 'on the gate', a task which involved opening and closing the gate at the right moment to admit only the sheep required, and so keep the clipped and the unclipped separated. Mr McNeill also drove out the sheep in lots when Rory had finished marking them. Mr Farquharson had the task of rolling up the fleeces, so each had his own exacting job to do, and in the glare of the sun, the men were all sweating freely, the younger lads being stripped to the waist.

Elspeth was kept busy, fetching flagons of water from the well, and she noticed that the whisky jar was no longer in evidence. She attached no significance to this, however, for the idea of drinking such fiery stuff in such a heat seemed ridiculous anyway. She had just returned to helping Rory when she heard someone remark in an undertone, "Here they come, lads!"

"Who's coming?" she asked Rory.

"The Exciseman – the Gauger," replied Rory, without looking up.

"The Gauger!" exclaimed Elspeth, dropping the tar brush she had been holding, as a shiver of apprehension travelled down her spine. But the men seemed entirely unconcerned. What will happen? Why doesn't somebody do something? What if the Exciseman should find a jar of whisky? These questions chased each other through Elspeth's mind, and her knees trembled so much she had to sit down on the turf.

When the Exciseman and his companions drew abreast of the sheep shearers the officer dismounted, and, glancing at some papers in his hand, he asked for Mr McNeill.

Mr McNeill stepped leisurely forward and the exciseman explained his business, whereupon Mr McNeill accompanied the party down to the farm.

Elspeth's heart was in her mouth, and it seemed an eternity before the men re-appeared. When they did, Elspeth was amazed to see them all chatting quite amicably together. Without more ado the Exciseman re-mounted and rode away.

The work at the buchts proceeded as if nothing untoward had happened, but, after a little while, Mr McNeill turned to Elspeth.

"Run up to the top o' the field, Elspeth, and tell us when ye see the Gauger's party turn into the main road."

At first Elspeth felt her legs were too weak to carry her, but she made her way up the field as quickly as possible, and, whenever she saw the horsemen cantering along the Alyth road, about half a mile away, she hurried back to the buchts.

Shears and fleeces were immediately set aside. The whisky jar was produced from its hiding place, and the men toasted each other, and congratulated themselves on another lucky escape.

"Aye, I'm thinking it was a blessing ye saw Willie McDougall's washing hanging on the line last night, Sandy," laughed Mr McNeill to Elspeth's father.

"To tell the truth, it's Elspeth we have to thank," Mr MacLaine grinned back, winking at his astonished daughter. "I'm afraid she did the good deed without realizing it. But cheer up, Elspeth. The danger's past."

So that was it! The line of washing had been the warning that the exciseman was on his rounds! And Elspeth realised that she had been right about the pony last night too, only it hadn't been a visitor. It had been her own father riding off to warn his neighbours!

When the last sheep had been clipped, and the flock returned to their field, the men gathered round the kitchen table again for supper. Their tongues had been loosened by the strong drink, and Elspeth soon learned quite a lot about smuggling from their hair-raising tales.

After the meal was over, Mr McNeill invited the men to join him in a game of cards.

"Yes, I'll stay, but I think you'd better go home now, Elspeth," said her father. "Take Ben with you, and tell your mother I'll not be too late."

Ben, who had been tied to a tree, to prevent quarrelling amongst the dogs, was delighted to be free again, and jumped as high as Elspeth's head to show his appreciation.

"I'll come up to the top of the field with you, Elspeth," said Rory.

As soon as they were out of earshot of their elders, Elspeth tackled Rory about the smuggling.

"Why didn't you let me into the secret?" she demanded. "Did you think I couldn't be trusted, because I was a Sassenach?"

Rory was taken aback.

"You know I wouldn't think that, Elspeth," he said reproachfully. "My father said we were never to discuss the smuggling with anybody, because you never know who may be listening. Besides, if your folk didn't tell you, Elspeth, it was hardly my place, was it, now?" To this Elspeth had to agree, however grudgingly.

As they reached the gate on to the moor, a spiral of smoke rising from a nearby hollow attracted their attention.

"Some of the tinkers must be camping on the moor," remarked Elspeth, as the tinkers often pitched their tents at this particular spot. It was in fact recognized as one of their camping sites.

"It's Blind Betsy," said Rory. "She was down at our place last night. Mother gets her to make heather besoms. You'll have seen her before, have you not?"

"I never even heard of her before," said Elspeth.

"But of course, you haven't been here so very long, and Blind Betsy hasn't been round this way for a year or two, Mother was just saying."

"But how does she get around if she's blind?" inquired Elspeth.

"Usually her man is with her. 'Besom Bob' they call him, because he makes heather besoms as well. But Betsy's not entirely blind. She's only blind in one eye," explained Rory. "My father said Betsy was the daughter of well-to-do folk up North, but after Culloden, the English dragoons took her father away and hanged him in the Tower of London. Then they massacred the rest of the family – all except Betsy. She was just a toddler, but she was wounded in the eye by gunshot. Some tinks found her, and nursed her back to health. They took her to live with them and then when she grew up she married a tink."

"My goodness! How old is she?" inquired Elspeth, mentally calculating back to 1746.

"About a hundred I should think, by the look of her," said Rory. "But actually, I suppose, she'll be about eighty. She certainly can't be much more. Well, I'd better be getting back. I have a lot of jobs to do yet. You'll be going to the Kirk tomorrow, Elspeth?"

"Yes," said Elspeth, "I expect so."

"Well, I'll meet you at your gate, same time as usual," said Rory, and with that they parted.

As Elspeth and Ben were passing the tinkers' encampment, a little black mongrel dog rose from it's place by the campfire as if to meet them. Suddenly it gave a howl of agony and drew back, holding up its right foreleg.

"What's wrong with your little dog?" asked Elspeth of the old woman who sat huddled over the fire.

"I think there must be a thorn in his paw, but my eyesight is poor and I cannot find any cause for the pain at all, at all," replied the old woman in a lilting Highland tongue. "It is sad I am for my faithful little friend."

"Shall I examine the paw for you?" Elspeth offered.

"That would be very kind of you, missie. The little dog will not be biting you. He is very timid, that he is."

Elspeth knelt on the ground and gently examined the paw until she located the cause of the trouble – a thorn lodged between two of the pads. As she pulled out the thorn the little animal whimpered, but, once the offending object was removed, it gratefully licked her hand. Then it scampered off after Ben.

"Thank you kindly, my dear," said the old tinker woman, turning to face Elspeth. As she turned, her heavy tartan plaid slipped back from her face, and Elspeth saw that she was indeed a very old person. One eye was covered by a patch, and the skin of her cheek was drawn and puckered, but the other eye was bright and keen, and there was an unmistakeable air of dignity about the woman which belied the tinker's apparel.

"You have the tongue of the Sassenach," remarked Blind Betsy.

"Yes. I was born in England but my father belongs to Glenisla and my mother's people were Scottish too. They had to flee from Scotland after Culloden," Elspeth hastened to explain, as she remembered how this old woman had suffered at the hands of the English dragoons.

"There is no doubting your lineage, my child," said the old tinker. "You have the proud air of the Highlander, and the Highlander's kind heart. Come, give me your hand, and I will be telling your fortune."

"But I have no money," said Elspeth, whose only knowledge of fortune-telling was what she had heard of the 'cross-my-hand-with-silver' habit of the English gypsy.

"You have taken away my little dog's pain, and that means more than money to me," replied the old woman, as she took Elspeth's hand in both of hers. "I have the gift of the second sight, but what I shall be telling you is for your ears alone. You must be telling no one, for there are those that say I am a witch and should be burned at the stake."

"I shan't tell anyone," promised Elspeth, almost in a whisper, for she was becoming decidedly nervous.

Betsy peered into the palm of Elspeth's hand with her one good eye, and traced the lines in the hand with a long, once elegant, finger. She seemed perturbed at what she saw, and gradually let the hand slip from her grasp. Staring into the flickering flames of the fire she seemed almost in a trance. When at last she spoke, it was as if she were speaking to herself.

"It is a difficult road you have to tread, for one so young. Aye, it is a road that is fraught with many dangers, and before the heather blooms twice on the hill, I see both flood and fire, and there are two dark strangers that are soon to cross your path." Here Betsy lapsed into silence, and appeared to be trying to unravel some mystery, for her face became tense and full of concentration.

"Nay," she said at last, "there are more than two. I see three shadows – three strangers – all dark strangers."

She paused, then continued slowly. "One of these you may think to be a friend, but he it is that is your enemy, and one that you may look upon as an enemy may yet prove to be your friend. The power is not given me to tell you which is which. Time alone will provide the answer.

"And of the third stranger I can only say this: he will cast a very dark shadow across your path for there is much evil in him. But hark ye now! I am hearing the sound of musket fire, and I am seeing the Shadow of Death! Aye, and the shadow of the gallows is there as well!" she announced in a horrified whisper.

Betsy, at this point, seemed to have completely forgotten Elspeth's existence, and recalling what Rory had just told her, Elspeth came to the conclusion that the old tinker had become involved with her own tragic memories. Betsy's head had fallen forward on her chest as if she were asleep and the silence was decidedly eerie. Elspeth began to move off, but, as she did so, the old lady looked up.

"It is an intricate pattern to be woven so soon round one so young," she mused again, "but kind friends are at hand, and the shadows pass. Remember, as long as I live you must tell no one what I have seen," and she raised a finger to her lips to indicate silence.

"I shall keep my promise," said Elspeth, but she was glad to get free of the old fortune-teller and to be on her way over the moor. It was a relief too, as she approached 'The Shieling', to see her mother waiting with the milking pails. Going about the routine jobs associated with milking time helped to dispel the feeling of unreality created by the strange words of Blind Betsy.

"Mother, do you know anything about Blind Betsy, the tinker?" she asked, as they sat together in the firelight when their chores were completed.

"Blind Betsy," Mrs MacLaine repeated the words slowly. "Yes I have heard the name before, but I can't say I know anything of the person. I've certainly never seen her. Why do you ask, Elspeth?"

"She's camping on the moor, and Rory was telling me about her," said Elspeth briefly. "By the way, Mother, I know about the smuggling now, and I know why Father was so interested in the line of washing last night. Why didn't you tell me about the smuggling, anyway? Surely you know I can keep a secret as well as anyone else."

"Yes, of course we know that, dear, but your father and I felt you were better to be ignorant of the smuggling as long as possible. Whisky-running is against the law and the punishments are very severe. The excisemen are always on the watch, and I can tell you it is all dreadfully worrying — especially for those who have to sit at home and wait. I wish your father would give it up, but it seems once a smuggler, always a smuggler. The excitement of it gets into their blood. Of course there are benefits to be gained, and there's no denying, we're glad of the extra money. It certainly isn't easy to earn a living on a Highland croft."

As she prepared for bed Elspeth thought about the events of the day. It had been a long day with many revelations. But the more she thought about Blind Betsy the more convinced she became that the old tinker's words were not a premonition of the future of Elspeth MacLaine. They were a re-living of the old woman's tragic past.

A Warning

The walk over the hill to Glenisla Kirk was always a delight to Elspeth, for she loved the Glen in all its moods, and today the weather gave promise of being warm and fine. She was up early, being awakened by a cock crowing from a gatepost near her window, and was soon dressed and downstairs, ready to lend a hand with the chores.

Instead of porridge for breakfast on Sunday mornings the MacLaine household usually had bacon and eggs; but today they had the trout which Elspeth and Rory had caught on Friday evening. After breakfast, Elspeth washed the dishes, while her mother heated the flat iron and ironed the clothes for church.

Mrs MacLaine's home in England had been on a large estate, where her father had been employed as head gardener.

There, when she was old enough, she had been given employment as a dressmaker. She had shown a natural aptitude for this work, and she now took pleasure in making attractive dresses for Elspeth and herself. Many yards of silk and velvet, and other fine materials, had been given to her by the wealthy ladies for whom she had worked, and often she had received cast-off dresses which were as good as new. All these she had stored carefully away, and though she had now been married for nearly fifteen years, she still had enough material to provide her daughter and herself with fine clothes for some time to come.

During week days, Mrs MacLaine and Elspeth wore the customary rough homespun skirts, but on Sundays Elspeth dearly loved to dress in her *braws*, as the local people called their best clothes. Many of the Glen dwellers were poorly clad, and some still wore the traditional tartan plaid as their main item of apparel, but Elspeth's love to dress up was not prompted by any desire to appear superior in any way. It stemmed from a natural love and appreciation of beautiful things.

"I think you should put on your lavender silk dress today, Elspeth," said her mother as Elspeth washed herself in the kitchen. "You're growing so quickly you'll soon be too tall for it, and it would be a pity if it were wasted. I've laid it out on the bed for you."

"Oh! good!" exclaimed Elspeth, "that's my favourite!" Climbing eagerly up the ladder, she could hardly wait to toss aside her workaday clothes and pull on her stiff petticoats before she carefully slipped on the rustling silk.

Standing on tiptoe on a chair she surveyed as much of herself as possible in the mirror which sat on top of the chest of drawers. Then she adjusted the wide lace collar at the neck, gave her hair a final brush and parted her curls in the centre, tying a bow of white ribbon at either side above her ears. This done, she opened one of the drawers of the chest and drew out the bonnet her mother had made for her. It was of a deep rich shade of purple velvet, not actually a poke bonnet but similar in style, and tied under her chin with black ribbons. She had white cotton stockings and black, elastic-sided boots, but these had to be carried, as it was the custom to make the journey through the heather barefooted.

A grey homespun cloak completed Elspeth's outfit and she knew she would probably need the cloak as they were to visit her grandparents – Mr MacLaine's father and mother – after church. By the time they returned home it could be quite chilly.

When she had her bonnet tied to her satisfaction, Elspeth put her boots and stockings into a draw-string bag and went down to the kitchen to watch for Rory.

A misty haze hung over the valley, but the sun was making valiant efforts to break through, and the little stone-flagged kitchen was bright and airy. From the open window a slight breeze stirred the curtains and the clucking of hens near the door made the atmosphere delightfully peaceful.

Elspeth hadn't long to wait for Rory. His approach was heralded by a bark from Ben who had been lying on the door step.

"Are you ready, Elspeth?" came Rory's voice.

"Yes. I'm coming," Elspeth answered, gathering up her things, and swinging the cloak round her shoulders.

"Don't forget your peece," called Mrs MacLaine from her bedroom, "and I put a clean handkerchief for you on the dresser, Elspeth. Remember to wait for us at the church gate."

Ben, who had trotted inquiringly back into the kitchen, wondering if he was to be allowed to go, now pranced out of the door at the recognized sign from Elspeth and dashed to the gate to greet Rory.

Having duly received Rory's few embarrassed words of appreciation of her new bonnet, Elspeth clicked the gate shut and they set off up the hill track accompanied by Ben, for, in those days it was customary for dogs to attend church with their owners.

"Did you see Blind Betsy last night, Elspeth?" asked Rory, as they paused on the crest of a steep incline.

"Yes, I did," Elspeth answered, and she told Rory about the thorn in the little dog's foot.

"Did she tell your fortune?" he inquired.

"Yes."

"What did she say?"

"I promised I wouldn't tell anyone what she said."

"Oh, well, in that case you'd better keep your promise," said Rory quietly, "for loyal Highlanders should never break their word."

By this time the mist had begun to drift away and the sun had broken through. Elspeth and Rory had reached the summit of the first shoulder of the hill above the quarry, and the track ahead of them led along the crest of the slope then dipped down to where a burn divided the hill into two parts. On the other side of the burn the path rose steeply to where green fields seemed to have been literally cut out of the hillside, and, at the corner of one of these fields, was a croft. This croft served as an inn to the travellers using the bridle path to and from Glenisla and was known as the Kirkhill Inn.

"Look! There's the others coming," said Rory, pointing back down the way they had come where they could see their parents, with Rory's two brothers, the Farquharson family, and several members of neighbouring families, toiling up the steep incline.

"Let's hurry, then," said Elspeth. "We want time to eat our peece." Off they ran, chatting and laughing as they raced each other down the slope to the burn.

Looking back as they passed the Inn, they could see their elders beginning the descent to the burn, so they quickened their steps and soon reached the iron gate through the march dyke which separated Glenisla from that part of the parish known as Kilry.

The journey, after that, was nearly all downhill and in the shade of a larch wood they sat down and ate their peeces with relish. Below them Elspeth and Rory could see the church and churchyard, the manse, the school, and the Inn, each little group of buildings almost hidden by a wealth of green foliage. Scattered around these larger units were various small cottages, looking, at this distance, like dolls' houses, some being clustered together along the banks of the Isla, while further away as far as the eye could see were farms and crofts and solitary shepherds' dwellings. From these outlying homesteads came many worshippers, some on horseback but most of them on foot. In fact, the Glen at this time on Sundays seemed to come alive with people.

At the foot of the hill Elspeth and Rory pulled on their stockings and shoes before crossing the footbridge. Once on the roadway they were caught in the stream of church-goers and hailed on all sides by those with whom they were acquainted. So they walked the last bit of the way with their friends and waited at the church gate for their parents.

The church bells had begun to peel by the time their families had joined them so they all went at once to their respective pews.

To Elspeth, used to the more ornate buildings of England, the interior of this little church amongst the hills seemed homely and welcoming. There were no magnificent stained-glass windows to give it colour, no decorative carving or fine tapestries, but in its very simplicity lay its charm.

The MacLaine's pew was upstairs in the small gallery, or loft, reached by a narrow stone stair. When she was seated, Elspeth could see through the window on her right the hillside they had just descended. Through the little window at the back of the church one could watch the late-comers from Brewlands, Fortar, and other places up the Glen, but most people were in their pews before the Minister mounted the steps to the pulpit. There was no organ, so the singing was led by the Precentor, and invariably the sermon was a long one.

Today, as his text, the Minister had chosen the words, 'And whereas ye appear righteous before men, yet inwardly ye are all hypocrisy and iniquity.' At any other time these words would have held no particular significance for Elspeth, but now, with her newly acquired knowledge of Glen activities, she saw in them a rebuke to the whole community, and she wondered if, like her, the Minister had just discovered the lawless activities of his parishioners.

Looking stealthily around her, she half expected to see her fellow members of the congregation blushing with shame and embarrassment or showing other signs of guilt, but no one seemed to take the words personally, and many were sound asleep before the text was given out.

By the time the sermon had drawn to a close, Elspeth was half dozing too. The quiet tones of the Minister, the twittering of birds in the churchyard, the distant bleating of sheep on the hillside and the murmur of the river nearby, all combined to act like a lullaby on a mind already drowsy from the long walk over the hill. She could feel Ben growing restless where he lay at her feet and she patted his head to encourage him to lie quiet, but she was glad when the Minister announced the last hymn and they were free to step again into the sunshine.

Little knots of people stood on the gravel path, or amongst the tombstones, discussing the happenings of the week, and the Minister exchanged greetings with each little group as he made his way to the Manse.

"Well, that's a fine day, Sandy," he greeted Elspeth's father. "Are you going to see the old people today?"

"Yes, sir. We're just on our way there now."

"Well you can tell them I'll be along later," said the Minister, "I'll see you all then too, I hope." With a pleasant smile to Mrs MacLaine and Elspeth, the reverend gentleman passed on to the next group.

The McNeills were visiting friends at Brewlands, in the opposite direction, so the two families parted, Elspeth and her parents going down the Glen a short distance to where her grandparents lived in a little whitewashed cottage near the main road.

"We didn't go to the kirk today, Sandy, because your father's leg was paining him," said Elspeth's grandmother as she welcomed them into the cottage, "and then, of course, I wanted to have a good dinner for you folk. I'm thinking you'll all be ready for it after that long walk across the hill."

And a very good dinner they had of Scotch broth, followed by cold boiled ham, potatoes and oatcakes, with stewed gooseberries and fresh cream as a pudding. When the meal was over they all went through to the sitting-room. While the older people discussed various local topics, Elspeth sat on a low stool and looked at a book. As she turned a page, an engraving fluttered to the floor, and her father bent and picked it up.

"This is Bella, isn't it?" he asked, turning to his mother.

"Yes, that's Bella," she replied. "They had that done when they were on their honeymoon. They eloped and got married in Dundee. Poor Bella! He certainly led her a dance!"

"Do you ever hear anything of the man?"

"The last we heard of him he'd been jailed for his part in the deer poaching up about Braemar," said Elspeth's grandfather. "Ye mind, of course, I put him out of this house when we discovered he'd had a hand in yon trap that was set to catch the smugglers up the Glen. A real dirty business it was."

"I remember hearing something about it, but of course I was in England at the time," said Elspeth's father.

"Oh aye, so ye were. Well that'll be about twenty years ago and we've never seen him since, though he vowed he'd have his revenge on us all. I don't think the man had ever earned an honest penny in his life. We were vexed with Bella at the time, but she was more to be pitied than laughed at. He cheated her like all the rest."

"Who was Bella?" Elspeth inquired.

"She was your auntie, lass," said the old man, "your father's sister. She met that 'good-for-nothing' when he came to work at the harvest in the Glen. He was a mystery man, and I warned her against him, but she wouldn't listen. She eloped with him when she was little more than a lassie and she died in Edinburgh before she was twenty-one. They said it was pneumonia, but we think she'd just lost the will to live."

"I wished I'd met the scoundrel!" remarked Elspeth's father as he handed the engraving back to Elspeth.

At that moment a tap on the door, accompanied by the

Minister's cheerful voice, put an end to the conversation, but Elspeth sat for some time afterwards looking at the two young people in the picture. She couldn't help wondering what had happened to the rather handsome young man who was her uncle, and who had turned out such a heartbreak to his young wife.

Tea was not an everyday drink in the Glen at that time, but was always indulged in on Sundays, and the Minister arrived just in time to join the family round the table.

"How did things go with you yesterday, Sandy?" he asked as he helped himself to a scone and raspberry jam.

"Oh, all right, thank you," replied Sandy MacLaine. "I saw Willie McDougall's washing line, by good luck – thanks to Elspeth here," he added, with a twinkle, "and so I was able to warn McNeill and Farquharson and the others."

"Well, it was lucky for all of you that I wasn't early in bed," said the Minister. "I just happened to hear the horses coming down the Glen and saw them dismounting in the Inn yard. They came over from Kirkmichael, evidently. One never knows which direction they're to take, these days. I couldn't even risk going to the glebe for the pony, in case that might draw their attention, so I just had to spread the news down the Glen on foot. I'm thinking you smugglers will be owing me something for shoe leather! In fact, the way things are going, it looks as if I'll have to retire from the ministry and take on the fulltime job of watchman!

"But, seriously, Sandy, I sometimes wonder if it wouldn't be kinder in the end if I took no part in it. Mind you, I wouldn't like to see any of you suffer for these pranks – least of all your innocent wives and children – but this cannot continue indefinitely. Something will happen which you will regret all the days of your lives. I must admit these violent clashes between whisky runners and excisemen which we hear word of have worried me somewhat. It is just a question of time before the same thing will be happening here. Smuggling is reaching alarming proportions in the Glen. And where would I be, think you, if the Presbytery came to know that I countenanced such goings-on amongst my parishioners?"

The realisation that the Minister was not only aware of the smuggling, but actually played the part of scout when the need arose was an eye-opener for Elspeth. The knowledge that this jovial man-of-the-cloth should be willing to take such grave risks for the sake of these erring members of his flock filled her with a deep respect. Obviously he was well aware that the whisky running, however unlawful, was to the Glen dwellers a vital means of ekeing out their meagre livelihood, so he did what he could to save them from the heavy fines or terms of imprisonment which such crimes incurred. No doubt, Elspeth mused, his timely warnings had saved many of the Glen folk from paying a heavy penalty.

"Do you always use the old bothy for your still?" the Minister was inquiring of her father.

"Oh, aye, I think its best kept a bit away from the house," said Mr MacLaine.

"But if the Exciseman came over the Kirk road and happened to smell the peat reek, what then?"

"Och! we have Tom McNeill's Highland bull in the sheep fank and nobody can get into the bothy without first crossing the fank, so I'm thinking there's very few strangers would venture inside," Mr MacLaine explained with a smile.

"You'll have some barley fermenting, then, I gather?"

"Aye, but we won't get a proper start to the distilling until the harvest's in."

"Well, Sandy, I came here specially to beg of you to give it up before its too late. I feel sure if you were to stop, many of the others would follow suit."

But Sandy MacLaine would make no such rash promises, and so the subject was allowed to drop, and the conversation progressed easily and pleasantly, to other matters of interest in the Glen until it was time for the family from The Shieling to take their departure.

Then the Minister said a prayer for the benefit of the old people, and they all joined in singing the psalm "I to the hills will lift mine eyes", so appropriate in that Highland community.

The MacLaines did not return by the Kirk road as it was a long, hard climb from the Glenisla side. Instead, they went down the Glen some distance, to where a ford crossed the Isla. From there they followed a cart track which led round the side of the hill, past various farms and crofts, until they came again on to the moor near Mosshaugh, about a mile from their own cottage. It was a longer route and involved fairly lengthy chats with several neighbours, but they eventually reached home in time for the milking.

Elspeth had been given much food for thought by the events of that Sunday. After she was in bed she lay awake for quite a time pondering over the various discoveries of the day and trying to think out the possible whereabouts of the smugglers' bothy.

The Bothy – the Bull – and Ben

All the next three weeks were spent in haymaking and sheep-clipping, and as the weather continued fine, good progress was made. The neighbours lent each other assistance with both tasks, and the hay was all cut with the scythe or the sickle.

Elspeth enjoyed the haymaking as there was lots of laughter and chatter amongst the workers, especially at mealtime breaks when they sat at the foot of the hay-cole and exchanged scraps of news and Glen gossip, or listened to the more musical members of the community playing tunes on a penny-whistle or a chanter.

Elspeth's job in the hayfield was usually to rake the hay into little heaps when it was cut. Then it was built into hay-coles by the men and women. After a week or two, it was carted into the haysheds to provide winter feeding for the cattle and sheep.

The next item on the programme was the carting of the peat for the winter fuel. It had been cut from the peat moss on the moor earlier in the year and stacked there to dry, so it only remained for it to be brought home. All the glen dwellers liked to have in a good store of peat and logs for the winter, and it was indeed necessary and wise, for winters in the Glen could be long and hard.

"Hey! You two! Have you forgotten about the blaeberry picking this year?" asked Rory's brother Lachlan, as they worked in the fields one day about the middle of August. "There's a really big crop over on the other side of the hill beyond the Kirkhill fields – far more than there is in the Den this year, I'm thinking."

"That's an idea!" We could go this Saturday, Elspeth, if the weather holds," said Rory.

"Oh yes! I'd love that," said Elspeth eagerly. So the matter was settled there and then.

Fortunately the dry weather continued, and they set out early on the Saturday afternoon, accompanied by Ben, each carrying a flagon to hold the berries. Elspeth had never been so far over the hills in that direction before, so she looked around her with interest as they crossed the Kirkhill fields and plunged through the heather. Very soon they found the berries, beautifully big ones, and deliciously ripe, so they set to work at once to fill their flagons.

"Just look at my hands," remarked Rory, after about an hour's picking. He held up fingers that were stained a deep purple.

"Look at your feet too," laughed Elspeth.

"You needn't laugh. Yours are just as bad," returned Rory. And they were, likewise her clothes, but both were suitably attired for the occasion, and so could afford to laugh at the blaeberry stains.

It was good fun at first, hurrying to see who could gather most in the shortest time, but after a bit the berrypicking began to grow tedious and the rest periods became longer and longer. At last the flagons were filled, however, and Elspeth and Rory thankfully threw themselves down on the heather. For a time they lay in silence, content just to enjoy the warmth of the afternoon sunshine, but at length for no apparent reason, Rory broke the silence.

"My father's Highland bull's in the sheep fank across there," he remarked.

Elspeth, who had been lying with her eyes closed, sat up with immediate interest.

"Where?" she demanded, quite surprising Rory by her enthusiastic response.

"Look, you can just see the tops of some trees over there," he said, pointing. "That's beside the fank and the bothy."

"The bothy!" exclaimed Elspeth, jumping to her feet, and shading her eyes with her hand. "That's where Father makes the whisky, then. I heard him telling the Minister about it on Sunday, and I couldn't think what place they were talking about. Let's go and see."

"There'll not be much to see," remarked Rory, who had no desire to spend the remainder of the warm afternoon plodding through the deep heather. "I've been at the bothy, but I never saw anything worth looking at." He lay back and rested his head on his clasped hands.

"Come on, Rory, you lazy bones!" cries Elspeth, seizing hold of his arm and trying to pull him to his feet, without much success. "Oh, well, you can lie there then!" she said at last in an exasperated tone. "Ben and I will go ourselves." She picked up her flagon of berries and plunged off through the heather, in the direction Rory had indicated, followed by the faithful Ben.

Rory watched her go, and, as she really seemed determined to visit the bothy, he at last scrambled to his feet, and called after her, "Wait, Elspeth! I'm coming!"

Elspeth pretended she didn't hear, and began to hurry, so Rory quickened his steps. Then Elspeth began to run, and soon they were both tearing down the hillside, helter skelter, yelling with laughter, until Elspeth subsided in a heap at the side of the stone dyke surrounding the sheep fank, and Rory, hard on her heels, and quite unable to pull up, came crashing down on top of her. Had the flagons not been fitted with lids, the berries would most certainly have been spilt but as it was, no greater damage resulted than a bump on Rory's head.

The sheep fold, or fank, had been built in a sheltered spot in a corrie beside a spring, and the bothy, a rough stone structure, with a thatched roof, a low door, and one small deepset window, stood in one corner of the enclosure. Sure enough, the bull was there, and no sooner did it become aware of their presence than it began to amble towards them in a threatening manner.

"He's not to be depended on! We'd better not venture in there!" warned Rory, as Elspeth clambered on to the top of the dyke.

"I'd like to have a look through the window and see just what is in the bothy," said Elspeth. "Look, Rory, you go round to the other side with Ben and attract the bull's attention, while I have just one peep. Please, Rory!"

"Don't be daft, Elspeth! It's not safe," argued Rory, eyeing the bull's massive build, and wide spread horns. But Elspeth persisted, and at last he unwillingly consented to go round the fank and entice the bull from the bothy so that Elspeth could peep through the window.

"You're mad, Elspeth! Really you are," Rory remonstrated, in a last effort to dissuade her. "That brute could toss you sky high, if he got you fixed on one of his horns."

"But I won't give him the chance, Rory. I'll just run across, have a look in at the window, and come back again. Besides, if the bull is watching you and Ben, he won't notice me. He doesn't have eyes in the back of his head."

"And what do you really think you'll see in one short glance like that?" demanded Rory. If you ask me, it's far too dark to see anything in there. You'd need to have the door open as well."

But Elspeth was not to be put off, once her mind was made

up. So Rory set off round the dyke side, with Ben barking beside him, and had no difficulty persuading the bull in the direction in which he wanted it to go. It was obvious that their antics had aroused its anger, for it began pawing the ground, rolling its eyes, and moving its head from side to side in a most disconcerting manner.

Rory didn't like the look of it at all, and peered anxiously over the dyke to see where Elspeth had got to. Ben, too, was wondering where his young mistress had gone. When he spied her running towards the building, he gave an excited bark. Before Rory could stop him, he had jumped over the dyke and was bounding across the grass towards Elspeth. The bull eyed the collie warily, for a few moments, then snorted wickedly, tossed its great horns, and began shambling after the dog.

"Elspeth! Elspeth! Look out!" yelled Rory frantically as he scrambled over the dyke and followed in the wake of the bull, heedless of his own danger.

Elspeth hadn't heard the dog's bark, but, at the sound of Rory's voice, she turned from the window, through which she had been peering, and was galvanised into action by the sight of the bull lumbering towards her. Swiftly she fled round to the back of the building, but was closely followed there by Ben, who seemed to think it was all a game. The bull, hot on the track of the dog, came thundering along behind. Could she reach the dyke, Elspeth wondered? As the bull came pounding round the corner of the bothy, she realised it was hopeless, and dodged round the front again. Then she saw Rory running towards her.

"Go back, Rory! Go back!" she cried, but Rory would not turn back now. He had armed himself with a thick cudgel and came panting on, while Ben, now sensing danger from the bull, turned on the enraged animal, biting its nose, nipping its heels, and somehow avoiding its lowered horns and flying feet.

Elspeth was terror stricken, and it was Rory who took command of the situation now.

"Run, Elspeth!" he cried, "Ben'll hold him!" As Elspeth appeared unable to move, he seized her arm and began dragging her towards the dyke.

The bull was now like a mad thing, and fiercely attacked the yapping Ben, who continued to bite its nose and its heels by turn, sometimes being bowled over, but, by some miraculous means, always managing to escape serious injury.

"He'll kill Ben! He'll kill him, Rory!" wailed Elspeth, now on the brink of tears.

"No! No! Ben'll look after himself," cried Rory as he pulled her to the dyke and half hoisted her on to it.

But Elspeth was quite overcome with concern for her pet.

"Ben! Ben! Here, Boy! Here!" she cried, almost in a frenzy, as she watched the scuffle from the top of the dyke. The faithful Ben, hearing her command, turned obediently. Catching him thus, off his guard for a moment, the bull charged, and, with a yelp of pain, the dog was caught on the massive horns and tossed in the air. Hardly had he reached the ground than the bull was on him again, and, to the horrified onlookers, the bull and the dog seemed to become one whirling mass.

Suddenly, Ben broke away, and streaked across the intervening space towards the dyke, but his previous agility had gone. One of his hind legs trailed helplessly behind him, and his attempt to jump the dyke was without success. He uttered a pitiful whine as if he realised the hopelessness of his position, and Elspeth and Rory immediately jumped to his aid. Hoisting him into their arms they somehow succeeded in getting him over the dyke, although the poor animal howled with pain in the process. Grabbing a stone from the dyke Rory threw it at the bull with all the force he could muster. It halted the charging animal in its tracks, and with one accord Elspeth and Rory scrambled to safety – not a moment too soon.

"Keep quiet," whispered Rory, as they all cowered on the other side of the dyke, with the enraged bull snorting and stamping nearby. The animal seemed to sense that they were still there, and repeatedly mounted the dyke with its fore feet, until Rory and Elspeth felt sure the stonework would collapse on top of them, but, at last, after much sniffing and snorting, and tearing up of the turf with its feet, it suddenly gave a loud bellow and began lumbering back towards the bothy.

"Quick! Let's get out of here, before it comes back," said Rory, and they immediately beat a hasty retreat, closely followed by the wounded Ben. In their anxiety to put as great a distance as possible between themselves and the bull, they completely forgot about their flagons of blaeberries.

It was obvious that Ben's leg was paining him a lot, and Elspeth was filled with remorse.

"It's all my fault. Poor Ben! Show me your leg, boy. There's a good, dog," and she hastened to examine her pet's injury as soon as they were a safe distance from the sheep fank.

Ben allowed her to inspect the leg, whining a little and licking her hand, but she had really no idea what was wrong with it. The poor collie had quite a number of cuts and bruises and was obviously suffering from extreme exhaustion.

"And to think I've caused all this trouble, just to see some tubs of water on the floor of that old shed," Elspeth lamented. Then she remembered about the blaeberries.

"I'll go back," said Rory. "We can't go home without them. You wait here with Ben. He looks as if he'd be glad of a rest."

"For goodness sake, take care," begged Elspeth.

"Oh, I'll take care, alright," Rory replied. We've had enough excitement for one day."

As he approached the fank, the bull seemed to get wind of him and began charging up and down, bellowing furiously, but Rory wasn't put off. Grabbing up the flagons he turned and ran, hoping against hope that the dyke would hold.

It was a very subdued trio that trudged home from the blaeberry expedition and when they were hailed by Mr McNeill from the bottom of the garden, where he was assisting

Elspeth's father with his bees, Elspeth and Rory poured out the whole story of their adventure.

"That'll teach you to mind your own business, Elspeth," said her father. "It looks as if you've had a lucky escape. If it hadn't been for Ben, things might have ended very differently for you."

Bending down, he carefully examined Ben's injuries. "I don't think the leg is broken. It seems to be dislocated, but he's dead beat, poor dog. You'll need to go across to the Smiddy and ask the smith to come over and have a look at the leg. Ben's certainly not fit to go any further."

"By jove! That proves what I said to the Minister, though," he said, turning to Mr McNeill. "There's nobody'll see what we have in the bothy as long as your bull's there." And to this Rory's father laughingly agreed, while the young ones went off into the house to tell their tale to Mrs MacLaine.

The blacksmith, who was gifted in the art of setting dislocated limbs, soon diagnosed Ben's injury and put it right, but the collie had been badly knocked around and he was very stiff and sore for several days – certainly not fit to do any work amongst the sheep. However, rest proved to be the only cure necessary and in no time at all he was running and jumping as well as ever – much to Elspeth's relief.

A Narrow Shave

The local sheep sales were timed to fit in between haytime
and harvest, and so the end of August saw all the farmers and
crofters gathering in their flocks. Most of the lambs were now
weaned, the best, or *tops* as they were called, being sent to the
first of the markets and the seconds being put into the fields
from which the hay had been cut, in order to gain extra
nourishment from the aftermath. Elspeth had a great interest
in the sheep and was pleased to help her father with them,
but it made her miserable to hear the ewes and lambs bleating
when they were separated. This year it was harder than ever,
for her father decided that her pet, Daisy, must now be put
with the other lambs.

"I've rented one of the parks up at Kirkhill, Elspeth," he
said, one day. "I'm putting the lambs – the ones I mean to

keep – up there, so Daisy can go with them. In a day or two she'll have forgotten about you, and she'll soon settle down."

But, although Elspeth knew the separation had to come sooner or later, she was not convinced about Daisy settling down, and she spent some sleepless nights listening to the distant bleating of lambs, and fancying she could hear Daisy's cry above all the others.

"There's bad news today, I'm thinking," said Mr MacLaine gravely as he came in from the moor one morning. "Tom McNeill, Geordie Farquharson, and Jim Brodie of Drumlea, have all discovered some of their sheep missing. We've decided to organise a search, so you can come along too, Elspeth, I expect Rory'll be helping as well, and the more the better."

"We haven't lost any sheep Sandy, have we?" asked Mrs MacLaine.

"No. Ours are all there Mary," Mr MacLaine replied.

"That seems strange, does it not?"

"Well, there may be some simple explanation, of course. Its possible the sheep have just strayed. We'll do our best to find them anyway." But somehow Mr MacLaine's words didn't sound too confident.

Tramping through knee-deep heather was tiring, even to those who were used to it, and Elspeth came home dead beat every night, falling asleep in a chair by the fire as soon as the evening meal was over. But, in spite of covering many square miles, and making exhaustive inquiries in neighbouring districts, no trace of the missing sheep could be found, and at last the fruitless search had to be abandoned.

"I'm afraid they've definitely been stolen," said Mr MacLaine, wearily.

"But why should they steal just one or two from various places, that's what puzzles me," said Mrs MacLaine. "One would've thought it would be easier to take a substantial amount from one flock."

"Aye, it would seem so, but this way the loss isn't discovered so quickly. Nobody can say exactly when the sheep went missing. If a large amount disappeared from one flock it would be noticed at once. Those men are crafty and cunning. It's a bad business, and apt to cause ill-feeling between neighbours, because everyone comes under suspicion. That's really the worst bit about it, I think, although of course, as you know, the loss of even one sheep means quite a slice out of a small income. I suppose we should count ourselves lucky that they passed us by." But lucky or not, Elspeth could see that her father was worried.

The fine weather, which had lasted for several weeks, now broke down, ending in two days and nights of torrential rain which opened all the springs, and brought the River Isla thundering down in spate.

"I'm glad we had the sheep gathered in, but I'm thinking this'll not help the look of them for the sale," said Mr MacLaine.

However, conditions improved a little, and, on the day of the sale, Elspeth rose to find the sun shining rather uncertainly from a cloudy sky. But, rain or no rain, the sheep had to go to market, and she and her father were ready for the journey early, being on their way before seven in the morning.

At this time, markets for both sheep and cattle were regularly held in the Glen on a piece of ground near the Glenisla Inn, and buyers came from far and near to attend the sales, for the Glen was famed for the fine animals it bred.

It was no easy business getting the frisky lambs started on the right road for the sale, but, after much shouting and waving of sticks, and much barking from Ben, Mr and Mrs MacLaine and Elspeth succeeded in getting them out of the bucht and on to the right track. Elspeth went in front, to lead the way, while her father brought up the rear, and Ben keeping a watchful eye for would-be stragglers, ran first on one side and then on the other.

As they wound their way round the hillside, taking the path by which Elspeth and her parents usually returned from Glenisla on Sunday nights, Elspeth could see other flocks coming from various directions and she felt excitement rise in her at the prospect of the busy market day ahead. Rory would be there, and also other young people she knew, and she was quite sure of having an enjoyable time if the weather stayed dry.

The Isla was still overflowing its banks in many places, and Sandy MacLaine had grave misgivings about the wooden footbridge they would have to cross, since the ford would be out of the question, but Elspeth, coming first in sight of the bridge, was able to report all well. Apparently they were not the first flock to go from that side. In fact she could see a previous flock in the act of crossing, and she wondered if perhaps it was Rory with the flock from Kilwhin.

At first the sheep from The Shieling were unwilling to venture on to the bridge, and indeed, it was not to be wondered at, for the noise of the flood was terrific, and the dark, swirling waters lapped the woodwork in a threatening manner, but, with a little persuasion, one inquisitive lamb at last ventured halfway, and soon the others were so eager to follow they were pushing and jostling as if each was determined to be first across.

A tall, dark, heavily-bearded man, was about to cross the bridge from the Glenisla side, with his two dogs as the flock from The Shieling approached, and he lent a hand to keep the sheep under control when they reached the north bank. All went well until one lamb, evidently terrified by the roaring of the waters, leapt right off the middle of the bridge into foaming flood.

For a moment Elspeth was horror-stricken, and stood staring helplessly at the animal in the water, then, seeing a rocky gorge where the water grew wider and shallower, she dashed down there in the hope that the lamb might be carried near the bank. Her hopes were fulfilled, and standing on the very edge of the bank, Elspeth neatly fixed her crook round its neck, bracing herself for the terrific jerk which she knew would follow, and shouting loudly for her father to come and help her. Alas, the bank on which she stood was already undermined by the flood, and, unable to stand the additional strain, it gave way, pitching Elspeth headlong into the swirling current.

The icy water closing over her seemed at first to rob her of her senses, but she was not hurt by the fall, and managed to cling to her crook which was still around the sheep's neck. Together they were carried down the river, and Elspeth found herself vaguely wondering what it would be like to be drowned, when all of a sudden, she felt herself grabbed by the shoulder, and wrenched out of the water.

"Let go of the stick! Never mind the sheep!" an unfamiliar voice yelled in her ear, as if from a great distance, and then she knew no more.

When she recovered consciousness, Elspeth found herself lying on some blankets under a piece of tarpaulin which was raised in the form of a tent. There was a strong smell of wood smoke clinging to everything, which made her cough and sneeze, and, after she had become accustomed to the smoky atmosphere, she realised that it was probably a tinker's encampment. She remembered quite clearly what had happened and she didn't feel ill, but everything swam round when she raised her head so she closed her eyes again.

After a little while she felt better, and raised herself to a sitting position. As she did so, a tinker woman looked through the tent opening.

"How are ye feelin' now, missie?' she asked.

"I feel fine, thank you," replied Elspeth. "I'd like to get up. Where are my clothes?"

The woman withdrew her head without answering and Elspeth heard her calling to someone. After a little while Elspeth heard a familiar voice outside and her father's head appeared in the opening.

"Are you all right, Elspeth?" he asked anxiously. "That was a narrow shave, you had, lass, and I couldn't get across the bridge quick enough to help you. It was lucky yon man was there. He pulled you out. Do you feel able to be moved now, Elspeth."

"Yes, I feel all right, Father, thank you. But what happened to the sheep?"

"Oh, it'll be none the worse of the soaking. The man's dogs pulled it out of the water."

"And where are all the sheep now then, Father? Is the sale started?"

"I think the sale will just be starting now, but our lot isn't due in the ring for another hour or more. Rory helped me to get them up to the market muir. He was on his way back to meet us and he saw the accident. I asked him to run down to your Granny's and tell her what had happened. So, if you're able now, Elspeth, I'll just carry you along there."

The tinker woman came and wrapped the blankets round Elspeth.

"Thank you very much for you kindness," said Elspeth, while her father recompensed the woman with a few coppers.

"I'll carry the lassie's wet things," offered one of the tinker children, who was hovering nearby.

"That'll be fine thanks. Then you can get your blankets back with you," said Mr MacLaine, and he set out to carry Elspeth to her Grandmother's house. Fortunately, a horse and cart happened to be passing as they reached the roadway and the driver hailed Mr MacLaine.

"Are ye goin' my way?"

"Yes. Down as far as MacLaine's cottage," replied Elspeth's father.

"I'll give ye a lift then. What happened to the young lass?"

Elspeth father explained about the accident as he set her in the bottom of the cart, and he and the tinker child walked beside the carter as far as his parents' cottage.

In no time Elspeth was in the warm bed her grandmother had prepared for her.

"What happened to the man who rescued me?" she asked her father.

"Oh he wouldn't wait. He said he was in a hurry, so he just went off, wet clothes and all. I asked the tinker woman who he was but she'd no idea. Now, I must be getting along to the sale."

"But I want to go to the sale too," wailed Eslpeth.

"But you haven't any dry clothes, Elspeth," her father pointed out. "In any case, you'd better stay in bed for a while in case you get a chill. I'll ask Rory to come down and keep you company later on. If you aren't able to walk home tonight you can just stay here."

Rory came down at the midday mealtime to see how Elspeth was, and to tell her about the sale.

"Did you know the man who rescued me, Rory." Elspeth asked.

"No. He was a stranger to us, Elspeth. We met him on his way to the bridge and my father asked him if there was a big turnout at the sale, but he said he hadn't been. It was lucky for you he happened along when he did."

"Yes, wasn't it!" Elspeth agreed. "But I wish I could have thanked him all the same. He must have got jolly wet, for the water was very deep."

"Well, I'll have to be going," said Rory, after a bit. "Our sheep are due in the ring just after dinner time and we'll be going home right away. That's to say if we sell, but I think we will, for the trade's fairly good, and there are two or three of the dealers keen on our lot. I hope we get as good a price as your father got for his. He seemed real pleased, Elspeth."

To have missed the sale was a very great disappointment to Elspeth, but by the time her father returned, her clothes were dry and she was dressed and ready for the journey home. She had received no severe bruises from the fall, so her aches and pains were few, and except for a slight cold, she suffered no bad effects from the ducking.

Alas! On the day following the sheep sale, a fresh calamity was found to have befallen some of the farmers and crofters on the south side of the Glen. During their absence their flocks had been raided and some had lost as many as half-a-dozen sheep. The losses had now extended beyond the immediate neighbourhood. In fact, most of the places in the

Glen were affected, except The Shieling, which alone could report all safe.

The MacLaines were, naturally, thankful that they had suffered no loss, but Elspeth knew her father was uneasy, and it seemed strange that they should be the only ones to escape the unwelcome attentions of the sheep stealers. Where the sheep could have been taken was a mystery and, owing to the vast amount of sheep tracks in the wet ground everywhere after the sale, it was impossible to follow any definite trail. Night watches were organised, but nothing materialised, and with harvest about to begin, the matter, for the time being had to be set aside, although sheep-stealing in the district was now attaining alarming proportions, and provided one of the main topics of conversation when any of the Glen people happened to meet.

The idea had been put forward that the tall dark stranger might in some way have been connected with the theft. Enquires were made regarding his movements on the day of the sheep sale, but he was reported as having been seen approaching Alyth later in the day with only his two dogs for company. So this clue, and further investigations by the Town's Officers, proved fruitless. The matter of the missing sheep remained a mystery.

Elspeth Sees a 'Ghost'

"You'd better get early to bed, tonight, Elspeth," said her father, as they sat down to supper one evening at the beginning of September. "Harvesting begins tomorrow at Kilwhin, so we'll have an early start."

And early start it was, with a long hard-working day, for all the grain had to be cut by hand, which was a lengthy business. Generally the men did the cutting with sickles or scythes, and they were followed by the women who bound the grain into sheaves, the sheaves being then tied with bands which had been made by the children.

Elspeth and Rory and the other children of the district, spent many hours in the fields making these bands, and helping to bind the sheaves and set the stooks. Setting the stooks was cold, wet work when there had been rain, but these people tackled the work with a will and saw no need to grumble. They were only too pleased to get the harvest in, in good condition.

But the harvest field had its lighter moments as well. The country people were full of humour, and there was always a great deal of laughter and joking, and many were the joyful rabbit hunts in which all the workers and their dogs enthusiastically participated, the dogs yelping excitedly, and the workers shouting and waving sticks as they leapt over the sheaves, or fell amongst the stooks. Quite often the rabbit escaped in the midst of the noise, but any such happy interlude was enjoyed by all.

At this time young men from the cities and towns often came to the country districts seeking employment at the harvest, wherever a farmer or crofter was in need of extra labour. Many of these young men were university students or school teachers, and their advent into the rural community was welcomed by the country people as providing a very pleasant change of company and conversation.

As such, Leo Cleeve came to the Glen. Being anxious to get the harvest in while the good weather lasted, Mr MacLaine and his neighbours decided to hire Cleeve's services for two months. During that time he was to reside at The Shieling, since theirs was the smallest family and they always had a spare bed in the house.

Leo Cleeve was quite good-looking, with a pale, intelligent face, rather bushy eyebrows, and long black hair. He was always pleasant enough but somehow Elspeth did not greatly care for him.

"He seems to be watching us all the time," she confided to Rory, "in fact, his eyes seem to be all over the place – almost as if he were spying on us."

"Och, Leo's not a bad chap, either," said Rory, "maybe you imagine it, Elspeth."

At harvest time, however, work occupied most of the waking hours, and as Cleeve was a shearer, Elspeth really only came in contact with him at mealtimes when, she had to admit, she found his conversation both lively and informative. Indeed during his stay in the Glen, she learned quite a lot from him for he was well educated and well travelled.

When the last load of grain had been safely gathered in, the Harvest Home dance was held in one of the barns or lofts, and all the neighbourhood were invited. This year the dance was to be held at Drumedge. Elspeth had never been to a dance, although she had been taught all the steps of the country dances by a dancing master who came to the school once a week after school hours.

"Please let me go to the Harvest Home this year, Mother," she entreated.

"Yes, I think you could go this time, Elspeth" said her Mother, "but we'll need to make you a new dress for the occasion."

Elspeth was absolutely thrilled, and every night when work was over, or when rain held up the outdoor work, Elspeth eagerly lent a hand with the sewing of the dress, stitching away under her mother's expert supervision.

The dress was made in the Empire Style, so popular at the beginning of the nineteenth century. Cut with a yoke, the skirt was gathered just below the arm pits, and there was a frill round the neck and at the bottom of the three-quarter length sleeves. The material was a dainty white lawn, with a sash tying at the back, and the dress, of course, was long.

Dressing for the dance by the light of a lantern was not very easy, but Elspeth was at last arrayed to her satisfaction, with her black curls tied back with a bow of red velvet. Then they all set out over the moor, with Mr MacLaine leading the way and Leo Cleeve making a fourth in the party.

When they arrived at Drumedge they found the cart shed lit with lanterns and quite a number of their neighbours already standing around chatting in little groups. Mr MacLaine and Leo joined one of the groups but Elspeth and her mother proceeded at once up the ladder to the loft, for the nights were growing very chilly and both wore thin dresses under their homespun cloaks.

The loft was also brightly lit with lanterns, and wooden forms had been arranged along the walls to provide seating, the walls themselves being gaily decorated with golden sheaves and autumn leaves. It was indeed a colourful sight, and seeing it all for the first time was a real joy to Elspeth.

"Hello Elspeth!" cried Rory, sliding down the floor, which had been polished for the occasion. "My ye're looking braw! I hardly recognized you!" He swung Elspeth round with him. "You'll be the Belle of the Ball!" he declared, gallantly.

"Now, now, Rory!" Don't you be turning her head!" laughed Mrs MacLaine.

When Mr and Mrs Farquharson, the host and hostess, came up the ladder, their arrival was heralded by a piper, and the farmer and his wife then lead off the dance with 'The Grand March'. Rory claimed Elspeth as his partner, and together they took part in nearly every reel and step dance that followed.

About eleven o'clock a break was had for supper, and Elspeth and Rory helped pass round the food. The local housewives had baked bannocks and scones, and there were the usual home-made cheeses, and several large-sized 'cloutie' dumplings, so a good meal was had by all.

"Who supplies all that whisky?" asked Leo Cleeve of Elspeth, indicating the collection of jars. "Do they have their own 'still' here, at Drumedge?"

"I never heard of it," said Elspeth, with a laugh, but she found herself wondering what would happen if the Exciseman should appear on the scene.

After the supper the fiddlers struck up again, and the fun continued, fast and furious.

"May I have the pleasure of this dance?" inquired Leo, bowing before Elspeth. As it so happened it was the fast-moving 'Broun's Reel'. Cleeve was inexperienced in Scottish country dancing, and becoming dizzy in the midst of the *birling* he completely lost his balance, pulling Elspeth down with him. As they rolled on the floor the other dancers roared

with laughter, and Elspeth laughed too, until she happened
to hear a schoolboy voice remark sarcastically, "My Goodness!
they can't even dance a Reel!"

"What could ye expect of two Sassenachs!" sneered
another.

"Aye, what could ye expect!" a third added.

Elspeth felt her face grow red with embarrassment, and
she felt an unreasonable resentment towards Leo Cleeve at
this unexpected revival of her hated nickname.

When Rory partnered Elspeth in the next dance, he could
see that she was in a bad mood.

"What's wrong with you, Elspeth?" he demanded.

"You know very well what's wrong, Rory. You heard what
those boys were saying.

"Och, I heard them, but why worry though they call you a
Sassenach? After all you *were* born in England, and what's
wrong with that?"

"Oh, I'm certainly not ashamed of being born in England,
but it's the way they say that word. You'd think I was a
traitor, or something. It's almost as if they were spitting on
me!"

"They just take pleasure in it because they see it annoys
you, Elspeth. Laugh it off, and they'll soon give it up."

Elspeth realised that Rory was giving her good advice, and
she was grateful for his kind words, but somehow she couldn't
regain her former good spirits. She declined to dance the next
dance, and once it had started, she collected her cloak and
went out for a breath of fresh air. There was no moon, but it
was a frosty night with a starry sky. As she wandered round
the steading, she became aware of someone a short distance,
ahead of her. The person seemed to be trying doors and
windows. Elspeth decided he was probably trying to find his
way to the dance.

"Can I help you?" she called.

For a moment there was no reply. Then a familiar, rather
puzzled voice asked, "Is that you, Elspeth?" It was none
other than Leo Cleeve!

"Yes, it's me," said Elspeth shortly.

"I didn't expect you to be wandering around out here all alone," said Cleeve. "I hope you were none the worse of the fall, by the way."

"No, I wasn't," replied Elspeth, rather ungraciously, "but I'm getting cold. I'm going in now." Before he could say anything more she turned and ran back the way she had come. The thought of what those boys would say if she and Leo Cleeve returned together, filled her with panic. Rory met her at the top of the ladder.

"I was wondering where you'd got to Elspeth! In fact, I'd begun to think you were away for a walk with Leo!" he remarked, with a broad grin.

"I hope nobody else was thinking that," said Elspeth, looking anxiously around for her tormentors.

"Och, no! I was just teasing you Elspeth! I think Leo must be away home to The Shieling, though. I haven't seen him around for a while."

"I know where he is. He's nosing around at the back of the steading."

"Nosing around? How could you see that when it's dark?"

"Oh, it's not pitch dark, Rory. Anyway, I heard someone rattling at doors and windows and I thought it must be someone looking for the way into the dance. It turned out to be Leo Cleeve."

"Maybe Leo was trying to find his way back to the dance, Elspeth, I heard your father saying that he thought Leo had had a bit too much to drink."

"I never thought of that," said Elspeth, slowly.

"Poor Leo! maybe I'd better go and have a look for him," remarked Rory thoughtfully. "It would be hard luck if he fell in the midden with his good clothes on."

"You needn't bother looking for him," said Elspeth dryly, "Here he is coming up the ladder." As she spoke, she quickly turned her head away from the approaching Cleeve.

Although they danced one or two more dances after that, Elspeth was quite glad when the evening concluded and the company gathered in a wide circle to sing 'Auld Lang Syne', and 'The Lord's my Shepherd' before taking their separate ways over the moor.

On the following Sunday the Harvest Thanksgiving was celebrated in Glenisla church, which was invariably packed to capacity for the occasion. Elspeth looked forward eagerly to the singing of the well-known Harvest Hymns. Decorations consisting of sheaves and Autumn flowers were arranged in the church for the service and Elspeth and Rory walked across the hill early to help with the decorations. After the service they also helped to distribute gifts of flowers and farm produce to the oldest members of the congregation and to the local poor.

By now Autumn was well advanced, and the countryside was a blaze of glorious colour. The mornings had grown frosty, and cold biting winds had begun to bring the leaves fluttering to the ground. Only the potato gathering remained to be done before the school session would commence once more.

During all this time Elspeth had thought very little about the smuggling, although she was aware that her father continued to be out late on several occasions, but the matter was brought forcibly back to her mind one misty moonlight night towards the end of the potato-gathering. Her father had gone off as soon as work in the fields had ended for the day, on the pretext of finding out about some stray sheep. When the household chores had been completed, Elspeth and her mother and Leo Cleeve had all retired early to their rooms.

Elspeth wasn't sleepy, and before starting to undress she sat down on the broad windowledge of her little window and gazed out on the misty landscape, lost in day-dreams. Suddenly, a movement below the window caught her eye, and she was immediately on the alert, but nothing appeared and she decided she must have imagined the movement. A little later, however, she was petrified to see a ghostly figure glide swiftly from behind a whin bush, and move rapidly across the moor. The progress of the figure was difficult to follow, owing to the indistinct light, the smallness of the window, and the fact that whoever it was took advantage of any available piece of cover. Elspeth began to shiver with apprehension. Who could it be? What could he want at this time of night? Her first impulse was to run to her mother's room, but, as the figure had disappeared completely from her line of vision, it occurred to her that the matter would be difficult to explain, and her mother would probably think she'd been dreaming.

Elspeth decided to go downstairs and see what she could see from the kitchen window. Silently she opened her bed-room door and slipped quietly down the ladder. But the kitchen windows revealed nothing more. There was no sign of life outside. Then it occurred to her that the figure she had seen might have been Leo Cleeve, and, on an impulse, she tiptoed to the door of his room. The door, however, was firmly closed, and since that particular door creaked when opened, she was sure she would have heard, had Cleeve gone out. Unless perhaps he had climbed through the window!

As quietly as possible Elspeth opened the outside door, and went a little way along the flagstones to look at the window of the other room but the window was shut and the curtains didn't look as if they had been disturbed. By this time she had worked herself into a highly nervous state, and when she suddenly heard the ring of a tackety boot against a stone on the moor, she almost screamed.

With a feeling akin to terror, Elspeth fled back into the house, closed the outside door and sped up the ladder to her room where she leaned against her bedroom door, hardly daring to breathe. Her heart was beating like a sledgehammer as she heard the outside door open, but it was only her father who entered the house, and she felt a surge of relief as she recognized his familiar step on the stone flagged floor.

Without more ado, Elspeth undressed and got into bed,

but when she heard her father at the top of the ladder, she called to him.

"What keeps you awake at this time of night, Elspeth?" he asked as he looked round her bedroom door.

"Did you meet someone out there on the moor, Father?" Elspeth asked urgently.

"Meet someone out there on the moor? At this hour? You must be joking, Elspeth!"

"I feel sure I saw someone on the moor when I looked out of my window," she persisted.

"Och! You'll be telling me next you saw a ghost!" laughed her father. "Get away to sleep, girl, and don't be imagining things!"

Sleep would not come easily to Elspeth after her alarming experience and she lay for some time, shivering with cold, and listening for any unusual sound. But she heard nothing out of the ordinary, and eventually she fell asleep.

Viewed in the light of day, the happenings of the night seemed much less alarming, and though she watched from her window every night for some time after that, she never saw anything of a suspicious nature, so the thought of the ghostly figure in the moonlight gradually faded from her mind.

The 'Ghost' is Laid

After the potatoes had been gathered, Leo Cleeve left the Glen, and The Shieling household returned to its normal routine. The smuggling now began in earnest, for the long dark nights supplied ideal conditions for such lawless activities. This was the time when strings of hardy little hill ponies began heading down the glens at dead of night, with kegs of whisky slung across their backs like panniers. Those sure-footed little animals, and their equally sure-footed masters, stepped out briskly on the rough mountain tracks, even in pitch darkness, but the light of the moon was a great asset for the transport of illicit cargo.

Elspeth kept begging her father to show her how the whisky was made. "Please let me come to the bothy, too, Father. I could do odd jobs to help you, just as Rory does for his father, and I promise I wouldn't get in the way."

Eventually her father gave in, and, much against her mother's will, Eslpeth was allowed to accompany him to the bothy.

She learned that the first process in whisky making was known as the 'malting'. The barley, already flailed, was brought to the bothy in bags, and, at this first stage, was put into tubs to steep until the grain swelled and grew soft. It was then spread on the floor, sprayed with water occasionally, and turned over several times. As a result, it began to grow, but, at a certain time in the process, the spraying was stopped and the growth allowed to wither. Next the grain had to be dried in a kiln, a stone-built erection built into a grassy bank, under which a peat fire was burned. This drying in the kiln was an important step, Elspeth learned, for the peat reek of the kiln combined later with other subtleties of flavour to give the Highland whisky its own distinctive quality. Having been dried, the malt had to be taken to a meal mill to be ground. It was then brought back to the bothy and mixed with warm water for the fermenting process. As the result of the fermenting, an alcohol-containing liquid was procured, and this was boiled and distilled. In the actual distilling, Elspeth found that the 'head' and the 'worm condenser' were the two main factors of the still, the former consisting of a broad-bottomed copper kettle, with a tapering neck, and the worm condenser being a spiral tube attached to the head by a short pipe.

The complete process of distilling had to be gone through twice and, even after the second boiling, only the first part of the distillate was pure whisky, the second part requiring to be mixed and boiled yet again with the next quantity of alcoholic wash. Consequently, the making of the whisky was a long-drawn-out procedure, requiring patience and skill. Elspeth was intrigued by the whole process, however, and never tired of watching the men at work. The journeys to the bothy were now almost always made under cover of darkness, and Elspeth soon came to know the various sheep tracks like the palm of her hand, and needed no light to guide her through the treacherous peat bogs.

One day, about a week before the school was due to begin, Elspeth was helping her mother to churn the butter in preparation for the weekly market in Alyth – to which Mrs MacLaine and other Glen housewives went, with baskets of butter, eggs, and home-made cheeses – when Mr MacLaine came into the milkhouse.

"I've decided to take some of the crates of honey to the market tomorrow, Mary," he announced.

"I was just thinking, Elspeth should go with us too, Sandy," said Mrs MacLaine, "for she is badly in need of new boots. The ones she has will never keep out the wet of that moor in the wintertime. I'm sure Rory would come over tomorrow and give an eye to things while we're away."

"That would be a good idea," said Elspeth's father, "but you'd better go and ask Rory now, Elspeth, in case he has other plans."

Elspeth was delighted with this turn of events, and eagerly ran to the stable to saddle the pony. Besides the heavy cart horse, which was used for the farmwork, her father kept two hill ponies, and Elspeth was a competent horsewoman, being able to ride astride, side-saddle, or even bareback when the occasion demanded.

Rory, as usual, was pleased to help out. "Of course I'll look after things for you," he said, in answer to Elspeth's request, and he arrived early at the Shieling next morning.

The visit to Alyth was, for Elspeth, something of an event, as she hadn't been in the town on many occasions, and she felt quite excited as they packed the marketing goods into the cart.

When all was arranged, Mrs MacLaine seated herself in the cart with the dairy produce, while Mr MacLaine walked alongside, and Elspeth rode the pony. This arrangement had been planned so that on the return journey, when the produce had been sold, Elspeth could sit in the cart with her mother, and Mr MacLaine could ride the pony home.

On Market Day, Alyth town square was a hive of activity as countrymen and women came from all directions to display their wares. Bargaining for the various items began early and the affairs of the market continued until early afternoon. After their produce had been sold the MacLaines had shopping to do for themselves, including the purchase of Elspeth's boots, and it was late afternoon before they were ready to leave the town and make their way to the Inn where the horses were stabled. Here they had ordered a meal to be ready for them before setting out on the homeward journey, so they entered the oak-beamed dining room and seated themselves at a vacant table. The dining-room was packed with country people and the atmosphere was close and stuffy. As soon as she had finished eating, Elspeth excused herself and slipped outside again, into the fresh air glad to escape from the noise and bustle to which she was not accustomed.

In the cobbled yard, the work horse from The Shieling was already yoked to the cart, and stood, munching from a nosebag, in one corner. Elspeth crossed and spoke to the animal. She was tired, and the night was quite chilly so she decided to have a seat in the cart until her parents were ready. Under some sacking the purchases from the town had been carefully stowed away and Elspeth also found some empty whisky kegs concealed in the bottom of the cart.

"This must be one of the inns that Father deals with," she said to herself, as she settled herself as comfortably as possible and wrapped her cloak tightly around her. Very soon Elspeth dozed, and at first, when she woke, she couldn't think where she was. It seemed strange that her father and mother had not yet come from the Inn, but she presumed that they had met some friends. She was just about to doze off again when subdued voices coming from the dimness of an alley, and the mention of the name 'MacLaine', attracted her attention. One of the voices sounded vaguely familiar, and, after a few moments, Elspeth recognized it as Leo Cleeve's voice. The speakers were moving in her direction, and at last came to a halt quite near the cart.

"I do have a fair idea where they have the still now," Cleeve was saying, "though I had the dickens of a job even finding that out. They gave me a room where the door creaked loud enough to waken the dead, and the window was too stiff to open more than half an inch, but I hid behind the meal girnel one night, and got out after the woman and the girl had gone to bed. Unfortunately it was misty, and MacLaine was almost on me before I realised it, so I didn't see exactly which way he came. Under the circumstances, of course, I was lucky, for if he'd had the dog, my presence would most certainly have been discovered. As it was, I got some nasty scratches from those prickly gorse bushes."

"They put plenty of kegs in the cart tonight, anyway, as you saw for yourself," said the other man, "so they're obviously meaning business, and I'm determined I'll catch that gang of smugglers yet, though it's the last thing I do. Somehow or other, they always get word of my coming but I've got a new plan. Listen!"

He began to speak in an undertone, and, inspite of straining her ears, Elspeth could not pick up everything he said. Piecing together what she did hear, she realised that this man was the chief officer of excise for the district, and that he had made arrangements for Cleeve to take up residence at Kirkhill Inn and spy on the smugglers in the neighbourhood.

"Get friendly with them," the man said to Cleeve." Invite them up to the Inn to have drinks with you. Have a game of cards with them. Let them feel they can trust you, and that you want to help them. Then, when you've found out as much as you can, give me the wink and we'll clear out the whole pack. Depend upon it, you'll be rewarded, and if you want to succeed in this profession, this is your chance to get your foot on the first rung of the ladder."

The two men continued their discussion about other places, many of the names of which Elspeth recognized, and then they parted, Leo Cleeve re-entering the Inn.

Elspeth was cold and stiff now, for she had not dared to move an inch while the men were talking, but it occurred to her that she had better leave the cart at once, in case Cleeve should return with her parents and guess that she had overheard the conversation. So she stretched her cramped limbs, and jumped down to the ground, where she stamped her feet and rubbed her hands to get back the circulation. Then she made her way across the yard and back to the dining-room. Her father was nowhere to be seen, but her mother was talking to Leo Cleeve.

"So there you are, Elspeth," her Mother said. "Where have you been all this time? I was just on the point of coming to look for you. Have you seen your father? I don't know where he's got to, and it's time we were away home."

At this point, Mr MacLaine appeared in the doorway and saved Elspeth the necessity of a reply. There were two or three other men with him and Cleeve immediately hailed them and started to chat animatedly as if he had been one of their best friends.

"I was just saying to your Good Lady that your Glen and your people have cast a spell over me, Sir," Elspeth heard him saying to her father, "and I've decided to spend a week or two amongst you before I return home. I intend travelling South before Christmas, but meantime I have arranged to stay at the Inn on the hill – what is it you call it? Kirkhill? – for at least a week. Perhaps you would be kind enough to take my belongings up with you in the cart, Mr MacLaine. Then I shall ride up tomorrow forenoon."

"Oh yes Leo, we'll take your bag willingly," said Elspeth's father.

"By the way," continued Cleeve, "I'd be very pleased if you and Mr McNeill and Mr Farquharson and their boys would spend the evening with me at the Inn tomorrow."

"That's very kind of you. Thanks very much. I'll see what the others say, and we'll let you know. Now we must be getting away home."

Cleeve hurried off to fetch his luggage, and then he accompanied them to the cart. Elspeth and her mother climbed in, the lanterns were lit, and Mrs MacLaine took the reins, as

Mr MacLaine was riding the pony. Then, with a "gee-up" to the horses, they were off, and had soon jolted over the last of the cobbles and out on to the rough country roads.

Elspeth decided not to mention the conversation she had overheard until they were safely within the four walls of their own home, so she curled up in the cart, and in spite of the jolting journey, slept most of the way out of sheer exhaustion.

Once inside the house, and seated at the fire which Rory had lit for them before he had gone home, Elspeth poured out the whole story.

"So you see, Father, I was right about someone being on the moor that night, and there was another time too – at the Harvest Home Dance, actually – I came across Leo Cleeve poking around at the back of the Drumedge steading. I thought it was strange at the time, but Rory said Leo had probably lost his way because he had had too much to drink. Now I feel sure Leo was trying to find out if Mr Farquharson had a still at Drumedge."

Mr and Mrs MacLaine listened with grave faces, and while Elspeth prepared for bed, her father continued to gaze thoughtfully into the fire.

"Aye, they've had it all cleverly planned," he remarked, at last, "but I'm thinking we'll beat them yet, Elspeth, thanks to you."

And, when she was lying upstairs in her box-bed, notwithstanding the lateness of the hour, Elspeth heard her father taking the pony out of the stable and galloping away over the moor.

Where her father had gone, or when he had returned, Elspeth had no idea, but she woke next morning with a feeling that a heavy load was weighing upon her and she remembered almost at once. Try as she might, then, she could not throw off the feeling of uneasiness which descended upon her, and she went about her morning's work with only half her usual enthusiasm.

"Cheer up, Elspeth," said her father, coming in to breakfast and seeing how troubled she looked, "we never died in winter, yet, lass, and this isn't the time to get downhearted. This is the time we've got to keep our wits about us. Now, in the first place, we've got a counter-plan and I want you to do something for us. After dinner time I'd like you to take Ben for a walk over the moor and up the hill and keep a sharp lookout for any move Leo Cleeve may make. He reckoned he'd be up at the Inn this forenoon and he must be kept away from the bothy at all costs, for there is no Highland Bull there meantime. I've no doubt Leo'll be scouting around to see what he can see, so, if you catch him moving in that direction just you show up casual-like, and keep him occupied until it gets dark."

"But maybe he won't stop for me, Father," Elspeth pointed out.

"Och he'll not barge past you, Elspeth. You must bear in mind that as far as he's concerned, we know nothing about his interest in the smuggling, and he'll not want to arouse any suspicion by showing an over-zealous desire to head in the direction of the bothy. He'll likely think if he doesn't manage to visit it today he'll manage tomorrow or the day after, but if you stop him this time, Elspeth, we'll do the rest. I'm sorry we've to involve you at all, but as I said, it is very necessary that Leo should be kept away from the bothy, and he is un-likely to think that it is a deliberate move on our part if he only meets you and the dog. You can tell him we're all willing to accept his invitation tonight and we'll be up at the Inn about seven o'clock. If you don't happen to see him on the hill, cry in at Kirkhill with the message."

Elspeth was too nervous to eat much at the mid-day meal and soon afterwards, she set off over the moor with Ben. Instead of taking one of the usual routes to the bothy, she made a wide detour, and, having satisfied herself that there was no one anywhere near the place, she made her way to a lone pine tree which stood in an exposed position and from which she could observe all the hillside between Kirkhill Inn and the sheep fank. Here she and Ben waited as patiently as possible.

It was a cold, raw, afternoon, with occasional drops of rain blowing in the wind, but Elspeth was not aware of the cold or of the loneliness, so anxious was she to fulfill the duty required of her. Carefully she scanned the hillside and wide stretch of moorland below but there was no movement of any kind, only the whaups wheeled and cried around her and the oyster-catcher gave its strange whistling call.

Darkness was beginning to close in when Ben suddenly pricked up his ears. Peering in the direction indicated by the dog Elspeth saw someone moving quickly through the heather below the Kirkhill fields. At that distance she couldn't be sure it was Leo Cleeve, but she rose without hesitation and hurried down the dykeside, emerging from a clump of silver birch trees beside the burn some little way ahead of the advancing figure which proved to be none other than he.

Elspeth fancied that Cleeve seemed slightly put-out at meeting her, but this impression lasted only a moment, for he quickly assumed his usual pleasant manner, and teased her about wandering on the hill on such a cold day.

"Were you looking for young Rory McNeill, Elspeth?" he asked.

"What about yourself? Who were you looking for?" returned Elspeth with spirit. "I wondered who the man could be, tearing along at such a rate. Maybe you were making for one of the crofts over on the Brewlands road, though? I saw you had your eye on Ailie MacGregor at the Harvest Home Dance."

"Was I really walking so quickly?" asked Cleeve, with carefully assumed surprise. "Well, I can assure you I had no intention of going anywhere in particular, or of seeing anyone, for that matter. Probably the cold made me hurry unconsciously."

"I'm glad I met you, anyway," said Elspeth. "I was coming to Kirkhill with a message for you from Father. He said that he, and the others you invited up for the evening, will be pleased to accept, and they will be up about seven o'clock."

"That'll suit me fine," said Cleeve, obviously pleased, "I hoped they'd come, for I feel I owe them some return for the hospitality shown me when I was staying at The Shieling."

"Oh, by the way," said Elspeth, drawing a small book from her pocket, "here's the copy of Milton's poems I spoke to you about when you were staying with us. Remember, I'd lent it to my Grandfather? You said you hadn't seen this edition. Well, I got it back last Sunday and I thought you might want to read it while you were on holiday."

"Thank you very much. I'll be delighted to have a read of it."

Elspeth immediately launched into a discussion about one of the poems. She hadn't wanted to part with the book but had thought it might prove useful as a subject of conversation and had slipped it into her pocket with that idea in mind. As she was speaking, she noted, with satisfaction, that the rain was beginning to fall in earnest, and the mist was coming down the hill.

"I say, we'd be better having our chat at the Inn wouldn't we?" remarked Cleeve, after a bit.

"I'm late enough already," Elspeth replied. "You see, I took a round about road to Kirkhill in order to let Ben get a good run, and if I don't hurry now, Mother will worry about me."

"I'll walk back with you," Cleeve said, after a moment's hesitation, so they set off smartly in the direction of the Kirk Road.

"Don't come any further," said Elspeth, when they reached the well-worn track, for the rain was by now coming down in torrents. "I'll run the rest of the way home. Besides, you'll get soaked if you don't hurry back to Kirkhill."

"I daresay you're right. Thanks for the book. I'll return it before I leave the Glen," said Leo, turning up the collar of his coat.

"Good night, then," cried Elspeth as she sped off down the hill, with Ben flying on in front. Now that her duty was fulfilled she felt she could breathe freely again. There was no fear that Cleeve would go to the bothy that night.

MacLaine was well pleased when he heard how things had gone. "I knew I could depend on you, Elspeth," he said. "I just hope our plan for tonight works as well." But what that plan was, he declined to say.

Elspeth would have been very surprised indeed, had she looked into the sitting room of Kirkhill later that evening and observed the behaviour of the occupants. Far from treating Leo Cleeve as the spy they now knew him to be, the men seemed to be looking on him as a trusted friend and joked and laughed with him as if he were one of themselves. Cleeve, for his part, was elated by the evident success with which he was to carry out the Exciseman's plan, and played the role of host with great gusto.

The evening passed very pleasantly all round, and as the company rose to take their departure, Cleeve led the way from the sitting room into the dark outer passage, holding aloft a candle. It was then but the work of a moment for someone to strike him a crashing blow on the back of the head and he crumpled up in a heap, never knowing what had hit him. Skilfully the men bound and gagged the unconscious Cleeve and carried him outside.

The Innkeeper had the two powerful horses belonging to the two Farquharson boys already saddled and waiting, and the limp body was hastily strapped across the back of one of the horses while the other had Cleeve's bag and belongings. Without more ado the two young men mounted, and, spurring their horses, rode off into the darkness of the hillside, while the other members of the party, having had a good laugh together, led out their mounts and departed to their respective homes.

Dave and Jock Farquharson didn't follow the usual tracks but rode as the crow flies, keeping a south-westerly direction first, and then swinging due south, making any detour necessary to avoid out-lying homesteads. In less that two hours they were approaching Alyth.

Fortunately for them, a close mist added to the poor visibility of the night, and they encountered no one as they rode past the sleeping township. Their destination was a two-storeyed house that stood by itself amongst some trees south-east of the town.

Dismounting a short distance from the house, one of the men reconnoitred the ground. As there was no sign of a watchdog, they speedily lifted Cleeve's still inert body from the saddle and carried him and his belongings to the very doorstep of the house where they propped him up against the door and beat a hasty retreat.

There, in the morning, the Exciseman (for it was no other house but his) found his plotting partner. As he opened the door Cleeve's body, bound and gagged, sagged at his feet. Naturally Cleeve was only able to give a very disjointed and unsatisfactory account of the happenings of the previous night, and he had no idea at all how he came to be on the Exciseman's doorstep.

The Officer of the Law was furious that his well-thought-out plan should have been so cleverly defeated by 'Those Highland Hooligans', as he called the Glen dwellers, and he vented his rage on the unfortunate Cleeve, threatening him with immediate dismissal from his service.

The Glen folk, of course, knew nothing of this, for the Exciseman took good care that the details of such an ignominious affair should not get to the ears of the general public. So the smugglers remained very much on their guard for the next few weeks, after which they began to breathe a little more freely. The Ghost seemed to have been well and truly laid – for the time being a least.

A Moonlight Ride

Elspeth wondered greatly at the sudden disappearance of Leo Cleeve, but when she approached her father on the matter he would only say, "Don't be too sure he's disappeared yet, Elspeth." So she just had to keep on wondering. She couldn't even discuss the matter with Rory since she didn't know if he'd heard anything about it.

Other matters began to occupy Elspeth's mind, however, for the end of October saw a return to the schoolroom.

The school in the Glen, like most other country schools of those days, consisted of only one big classroom and every pupil in that room was taught by one teacher – known locally as the Dominie. The age groups ranged from five-year olds to young men in their late teens whose lives were governed by the work requirements at home. Their only hope of acquiring an education was to return to the schoolroom, for the winter term only, year after year right up to manhood.

Elspeth enjoyed her school lessons, but inevitably, her hated nickname was resurrected and this tended to spoil things for her. However, with Rory ever ready to champion her cause when necessary, school life gradually settled into its normal routine.

The work of the smuggling community had returned to its normal pattern but Elspeth's and Rory's visits to the bothy were now restricted to the weekends. Then, one Friday, while the MacLaine family were busy at their evening meal, an unexpected messenger, in the form of young Henry the ostler at Kirkhill Inn, arrived at The Shieling. He had come with the news that an Exciseman's raid was pending. Apparently a traveller from Kirkmichael had passed the Exciseman's party dismounted at a farm, and had hastened to Glenisla to warn the Glen folk. They in turn had sent word to Kirkhill, and now Henry was on his way to give a timely warning to the smugglers on the south side of the Glen.

"By jove, this suits my purpose admirably," declared Mr MacLaine when Henry had gone. "I'll get those kegs delivered to Alyth without the risk of meeting the Gauger on my way down," and he saddled the larger of the two ponies and rode off to the bothy, where, having hidden all incriminating evidence, he strapped the kegs of whisky across the pony's back and set out for Alyth.

Mr MacLaine had only been on his way about half-an-hour when Elspeth and her mother caught the sound of galloping hoofs coming towards The Shieling and, with one accord, they rushed to the door. Over the moor came a brown and white pony which both recognised as belonging to the Minister, and, indeed, it was.

"Is the goodman in?" he asked anxiously, as he reigned in the pony at the gate.

"No. He's gone to Alyth just a little while ago," Mrs MacLaine replied.

"Just what I feared," said the reverend gentleman

agitatedly, removing his broad-brimmed hat and mopping his brow with a monstrous white handkerchief. "I came as quickly as I could, but I feared I might be too late to catch Sandy before he left. I knew he was meaning to run some contraband through to Alyth this week and I guessed how he'd react to the news about the Gauger. Well, I'm sorry to say the news was false. I came down from Kirkmichael myself not an hour afterwards and there was no sign of any excisemen. Worse than that," continued the Minister, "news was awaiting me at the manse, from my friend in Alyth who keeps me informed on the movements of the Excise, that the Gauger and his henchmen were to leave the town in the late evening. They intend to make a trip up the Glen by moonlight tonight. I'm afraid the kind traveller who pretended to be so helpful had been in the employment of the Gauger. And goodness knows how many more of my parishioners will react as Sandy has done. Truly, Mrs MacLaine, the strain of trying to keep my flock out of trouble is making an old man of me!"

"I know! I know how worrying it is!" cried Mrs MacLaine distractedly, "and I have begged Sandy to give up the smuggling. But what are we to do now? Sandy will ride straight into the trap."

"Don't you worry, Mother," cried Elspeth at this point. "We've still time! I'll ride after father!" Turning on her heel she dashed back into the kitchen and up the ladder to her room. Hastily she changed into the riding breeches which her mother had made for her so that she could ride astride the pony on the treacherous moorland tracks.

She looked very slim and boyish in this outfit and the Minister gasped in amazement as she came bounding down the ladder into the kitchen, where Mrs MacLaine was serving him a hot drink. But there was no time for joking.

"Wrap yourself up well, Elspeth," cried her Mother anxiously, as Elspeth raced to the stable to saddle the pony.

In no time she was ready, and jumping lightly into the saddle at the gate, she was off over the moor, thankful for the full moon which made the country almost as bright as day.

Down past the smiddy at breakneck speed went the flying forms of Elspeth and the pony disappearing between the high banks of the narrow roadway before the inhabitants of the various cottages had time to do more than unbolt their doors.

Turning into the main road they continued at full gallop past the Standing Stone and over the ford of the Kilry Burn. On the next rise Elspeth slackened speed and headed the pony off the main Alyth road into a side track. This was a short cut, but the ruts in the path were treacherous and there were many loose boulders which made speed impossible. She anxiously scanned the terrain in front but still there was no sign of her father, and, as soon as they had negotiated the worst of the track, she urged the pony once more to a trot. They continued thus until they began the long, steep ascent of the Alyth Hill. Here Elspeth dismounted and pressed forward on foot.

There was no time to feel nervous, although the track they followed led through thick woodlands that were ghostly in the moonlight, and over open spaces dotted here and there with weirdly shaped bushes of broom and whin. Occasionally Elspeth started when an owl screeched eerily overhead, and sometimes when the bleat of a solitary lamb sounded like a human cry, she would feel a cold shiver run down her spine. But for the most part she paid little attention to those sounds of the night, keeping her eyes glued to the path in front, and hoping against hope that she would be in time to prevent her father falling into the hands of the Exciseman.

A feeling of hopelessness began to take hold of Elspeth, as she breasted the last slope of the hill. How could she ever hope to overtake her Father now? Then suddenly, in the shadow of the trees, just ahead of her, she heard a shuffling of dead leaves, and the unmistakeable sound of an iron-shod hoof striking against a stone. Then the dark forms of a horse and rider were, for a moment, silhouetted against the skyline.

"Father!" she called urgently, and heard her father swear under his breath.

"Elspeth! What, in the name of goodness, are you doing here?" her father exclaimed, in an exasperated whisper.

"I came to warn you," panted Elspeth, as she drew alongside him. "The message about the Gauger was false. He's on his way up from Alyth now."

"Surely not! Well, by jove, it's time we were out of here! I was observing a party of riders coming up the track just before you spoke and I could have sworn it was the Gauger himself, but naturally I thought I must be mistaken. Look, you can see them now, just at that bend in the track. Come on, lass, we've no time to lose, for I'm sure they've seen me too."

So saying, Mr MacLaine turned his horse into the trees to the left of the track, and leapt into the saddle, signing to Elspeth to follow him, which she did with alacrity.

Down the steep slope they slithered, the hardy hill ponies scarcely managing to keep their feet. At the bottom Mr MacLaine set his horse to a gallop, out into the open, making for a thick belt of trees which were just visible over a hillock to the south west.

Since Elspeth had no load on her pony it covered the ground more easily than her father's and she reached the shelter of the trees first. Before Mr MacLaine had time to join her, a yell sounded in the direction from which they had come, and her father gave an exclamation of annoyance.

"They've seen me. Dammit! Quick, Elspeth, go through the wood to the right there! I've got a plan, but we'll need time to put it into action, and that gang'll be on us in a wink, for their horses are fresh. There's one thing, though, they've no idea you're with me."

When they reached the other side of the wood, Mr MacLaine swiftly dismounted. "Here, Elspeth, you take Prince and give me Rusty, but first help me to tie some clumps of heather to Rusty's saddle."

Somehow or other they succeeded in gathering fairly bulky bunches of heather and broom and these Mr MacLaine hastily tied to Rusty's saddle, giving Elspeth hasty instructions as he did so.

"Take cover behind the thick undergrowth over there, he directed. "I'll ride out over the hill in the Airlie direction. You stay put until the coast is clear, then make a beeline for Alyth with the cargo. You know which Inn it is. You've been there. If you don't see the landlord, just dump the kegs and come away. "He'll know they're from me. I wouldn't have had you mixed up in this for the world, Elspeth, but what's done can't be undone. Whatever you do, don't let the Gauger's party see you or we're done for. Take care of yourself, lass, and good luck!"

So saying, her father mounted the pony and rode boldy out into the open while Elspeth led Prince into the hiding place her father had indicated, and waited to see what would happen.

They were not a moment too soon, for even as her father was issuing his instructions they could hear their pursuers shouting to each other as they searched the far side of the wood.

As she watched her father galloping over the hillside, Elspeth could see that his trick had been a good one, for the bushy clumps on either side of the saddle certainly resembled panniers. Their pursuers must have thought so too, for, as soon as they caught sight of the flying horseman, they immediately gave chase. Four of them in all, Elspeth counted, and then she turned Prince's head in the opposite direction and led him, as quickly as possible, over the brow of the hill towards the twinkling lights of the town, taking advantage of any cover that might present itself.

Luck seemed to be in her favour, for the moon suddenly sailed behind a cloud, rendering the landscape more indistinct, and Elspeth took courage from the darkness and pressed on towards Alyth.

As she approached the houses on the outskirts of the town her courage wavered a little, and she peered nervously about her, feeling like a criminal, and fancying that unseen eyes were watching her every movement. She longed to jump on the pony's back and head for home but she knew she must deliver her load, and also preserve a calm exterior so as not to arouse suspicion. It was with a sense of relief that she at last saw the dark outline of the Inn loom up in front of her.

Elspeth led the pony in by a back entrance, but, as she was crossing the Innyard, a door was thrown open and the figures of two men were silhouetted against the light. They came out into the yard, and Elspeth hurriedly drew back into the shadows, but the men had not seen or heard her, and they themselves appeared so furtive in their movements and so anxious to be off that Elspeth felt sure they must have been on the same unlawful mission as she was. Nevertheless, she heaved a sigh of relief when they had ridden away, and she remained trembling where she was until the door opened again and a man in shirtsleeves, whom she recognized as the Innkeeper, came out carrying some empty crates. As he was stacking the crates against a wall, Elspeth stepped out of the shadows and approached him. The poor man started visibly, and seemed about to beat a retreat, but Elspeth addressed him by name and he waited for her to draw near.

"My, what a fright ye gave me, laddie," he exclaimed, mistaking Elspeth's trouser-clad figure for that of a boy. "But who are ye?" he enquired, peering into her face. "I don't think I know ye."

Elspeth explained who she was, and the man laughed.

"Jove! ye'd make a fine young lad, in that outfit. The lassies would be fallin' for ye, and that's for sure, but what's wrong wi' your father, lass, that he should be sendin' you out on such a ploy at this time o' night?"

Elspeth looked around to make sure she wouldn't be overheard and then briefly outlined what had happened.

The Innkeeper laughed. "My, yon lads are not easy beat. They're up to all the dodges," he said, "but step into the kitchen there, Elspeth, and my wife'll give ye something to warm ye up while I unload the kegs you've brought," and he ushered Elspeth through the doorway, calling to his wife to come and prepare some supper.

The Innkeeper's wife, a big jovial woman, with a smiling

face like her husband's, welcomed Elspeth without any questions and soon set a hearty supper before her, but Elspeth was still too nervous to feel inclined to eat, and did little more than taste the food.

"Would ye not like me to send somebody back with ye?" asked the Innkeeper, when he joined them in the kitchen. "It's a long lonely road for ye by yourself, and the night's getting late."

But Elspeth had no fear of the homeward journey, only a feeling of relief that she had safely carried out her father's instructions, so she was quite adamant regarding an escort.

"No, no thank you," she replied, "I'm not frightened when I'm on the pony, and I shan't take long. Besides, its nice and clear in the moonlight."

So the Innkeeper accompanied her outside and held the pony while she mounted. Then, having thanked the couple for their hospitality, Elspeth bade them goodnight and set out for home.

She was glad to be clear of the town and once out in the country again she made good headway, the sure-footed Prince mounting the hill like a roedeer. The moon was still bright as they began the descent of the other side and now everything seemed so calm and peaceful that Elspeth found it difficult to imagine that, only a few hours before, her father and she had galloped over the same ground as fugitives in search of a hiding place.

Quite suddenly the peace of the night was broken by the distant bleating of sheep. Elspeth reined in her pony and listened intently. As she did so she became aware of the dark forms of men and horses moving silently up the hillside towards her.

"The Gauger!" gasped Elspeth. Panic stricken, she headed Prince towards the wood. Quickly dismounting she led the pony into the shelter of the trees and waited with bated breath for the approaching party. But as the cavalcade passed her hiding place she heaved a sigh of relief. It was a party of smugglers heading south with their whisky kegs slung across the ponies' backs. Obviously, as the Minister had predicted, more of the whisky-runners had reacted in the same way as her father!

Just as Elspeth was about to move out on to the path again she caught a glimpse of sheep moving quickly along the hillside. The white of the fleeces stood out in the moonlight and she could see there was quite a large flock. Something warned Elspeth to remain hidden so she watched the progress of the flock from the shelter of the wood.

Two dogs, both of which seemed to strike a vague chord in Elspeth's memory, were handling the sheep with great dexterity, and, from the time they came into her line of vision until they passed her hiding place, Elspeth heard no word of instruction being issued by their master. She watched in admiration as the collies worked like two silent shadows, never uttering a yelp or a bark but keeping the sheep under perfect control as the flock hurried on its way. Then, by mere chance, Elspeth's eye was caught by something familiar about one of the sheep. Forgetting her need to remain hidden, she took a step forward, almost betraying her presence in her desire to see the sheep again, but it was lost to view. Nevertheless, Elspeth felt positive that in that brief glimpse she had seen the head and crumpled horn of Rory's old pet, Crumpie. And, as the drovers came into view, she realised why the dogs had seemed familiar. One of the drovers was the tall dark stranger she had met on the day of the sheep sale – the man who had rescued her from the river.

For a few minutes after the men and their flock had passed out of her sight, Elspeth stood stock still, her mind in a turmoil. Rory had never said he had sold Crumpie, and there hadn't been a sheep sale lately, at least as far as she knew. Could Crumpie have been stolen? If so, why hadn't Rory mentioned it? Of course it was possible that another sheep could have a similar twist on its horn. Finally, she decided it would better to say nothing about seeing Crumpie until she had spoken to Rory.

A mile or so further on, Elspeth's mount raised its head

and whinnied enquiringly while an answering neigh came from the shadow of some trees nearby. Elspeth clutched the reins nervously and drew the pony to a halt, but her father's voice reassured her.

"Come away, Elspeth," he called. It's only Rusty and me."

Elspeth felt such a surge of relief at the sound of his voice she nearly burst into tears. It was only then that she began to realise how great had been the strain of the last few hours.

Elspeth was anxious to know how her father had fared since they parted, and eagerly questioned him as she joined him beside the stream where Rusty was quenching his thirst.

"Did they catch you, Father?"

"I doubt I wouldn't be here if they had, Elspeth."

"But then they couldn't have convicted you, when you only had two bunches of heather tied to the saddle," Elspeth pointed out.

"Maybe so, but they certainly wouldn't have allowed me to get off scot free after my leading them such a dance. Anyway, I'm glad to say, they didn't catch me, and I don't think they got near enough to identify me either."

"Which way did you go, Father?"

"I headed for the Den of Airlie, as I said I would, and they lost me there, so I doubled back towards the Slug of Auchrannie and the Reekie Linn, where there's plenty of cover. I lay low there for a bit, and, when I saw them making off in the direction of the Knock of Formal, I knew they'd given up the chase and I came back here to wait for you. Now, what about your side of the story, Elspeth?"

Elspeth described her share in the evening's escapade. Then she told her father about the smugglers, and asked if he'd seen any sheep going over the hill.

"The sheep didn't pass here, Elspeth, but I thought I heard some in the distance. Did you see them?"

"Yes, I did. Where could they have been going at this time of night?"

"Oh, it's not unusual for folk to take the chance of the

moonlight to drove their sheep or cattle to the market, Elspeth. More than likely there'll be a sheep sale in Blairgowrie or Coupar Angus tomorrow. Did you see which way they came?"

Elspeth described where she had seen the sheep join the path she was following.

"Aye, they would be from Shealwalls likely. How many folk were droving them?"

"Two men, and I'm sure one was the man who rescued me from the river. You don't think the sheep had been stolen, do you, Father?" she felt forced to ask.

"I don't think so, Elspeth. I know who the men would be, although I don't know them personally. They're brothers. MacKeracher is the name and they live near Burrelton. They're sheep and cattle dealers and they've been buying a lot of sheep around this area recently. In fact, they were up seeing Tom McNeill just yesterday, I believe. Angus MacKeracher was the man that rescued you and it was his dogs that saved the lamb. They certainly are marvellous dogs. I'm told they're a brother and sister team and there's simply nothing to compare with them anywhere around.

"Not even Ben?"

"No, not even Ben," laughed her father, "but Ben's a good dog all the same. Well, the horses should be refreshed now, Elspeth, so we'd better get away home."

So they mounted again and rode on, talking but little, for they were both tired after the exertion and strain of a very long night. Elspeth, for her part, was much relieved by her father's words regarding the flock of sheep. She would have hated to think that her hero of the hour – the man who had so gallantly saved her life – should have turned out to be nothing more than a common thief. But there was still the matter of Crumpie . . .

A Peck of Troubles

School had been continuing much as usual for a few weeks,
and November was now well on its way. With a renewal of
the dancing class Elspeth began to enjoy herself more, for she
loved dancing, and was considered one of the best dancers
amongst the girls. Consequently the older boys were always
keen to partner her, and the hated nickname was more-or-
less dropped for a time, since she always refused to dance
with those who called her the Sassenach. Elspeth began to
hope that they would forget about it altogether, but her
hopes were short-lived, for troubles were brewing of which
she knew nothing and rumours regarding the sheep stealing
were growing in magnitude. As is often the case the chief
parties concerned were entirely ignorant of the evil tales.

Realisation of what was in the minds of some of their

neighbours came to Elspeth one wet, windy night as she and several other pupils made their way homeward after the dancing class. A quarrel had arisen about the high marks Elspeth had received in an exam that day and one boy accused her of cheating, which Elspeth vehemently denied. Matters went from bad to worse, until someone alluded to the disappearace of so many sheep in the district.

"It's funny everbody's had sheep stolen except you folk," was the sneering remark.

"Aye, that's the worst of Sassenachs coming to live in the Glen," added another.

"And how do you and your father happen to be riding about at all the hours of the night, tearing past folks doors as if you were terrified you'd be seen?" demanded a third.

Elspeth was completely shattered at the implication which these words held. Since most of the Glendwellers were smugglers themselves they would not be insinuating anything regarding the traffic in whisky. There was only one explanation – they suspected the MacLaines of being involved in the sheep stealing!

Rory had not stayed for the dancing class that evening so she had no one to turn to for reassurance, and she felt quite sick inside when she left the others and was crossing the darkening, windswept moor by herself. Even the welcoming light from the window of The Shieling was not enough to cheer Elspeth's sinking heart.

But Elspeth's own worries were quickly banished when she stepped into the kitchen of her home. One glance at her mother's face was enough to tell her that something was wrong, and the sight of an open travelling truck beside the fireplace gave her quite a shock.

"What's happened," she cried anxiously.

"Your English grandfather is ill," said her father quietly. "Look, there's the letter on the mantelshelf, Elspeth. Read it for yourself. Your Mother has to go south tomorrow."

Elspeth hurriedly read the letter which her grandmother had sent. It was short and to the point, containing only the news that Mrs MacLaine's father was very ill, and that her mother felt she should come home as the old man was asking for her.

"Oh, Mother, I'm so sorry!" exclaimed Elspeth, giving her a sympathetic hug. "What can I do to help you?"

"Just carry on as usual, Elspeth," said her mother quietly, "I shall have to leave all my duties to you while I'm away, you know."

As Elspeth sat down to her meal, her mother continued with her packing, giving Elspeth various instructions as she did so. Later Elspeth did all the milking by herself and her father came out to her in the byre.

"I've been thinking, Elspeth, I can't let your mother go all that long journey alone," he said. "I must go with her. I'll ride up the Glen tonight and ask your Granny and Grandfather to come for a week or two to be here with you till we see how things go down south. You'll manage every thing, I'm sure. There's not much to be done at the bothy meantime. I have some barley steeping, but Tom McNeill will take what is ready for bruising to the miller when he is taking his own. The Alyth Inn will just have to wait till I come back for their next supply. If a storm comes – which I hope it won't – bring the sheep down from Kirkhill to one of our own fields. Your Grandfather'll be able to advise you, though he's not able to walk so far now, and I'm sure Farquharson or McNeill will be pleased to lend a hand if necessary. You'll have to stay off school, and I'm sorry about that, Elspeth, but you'll soon catch up again when we get back."

Elspeth, with a confidence she was far from feeling, promised to do everything to the best of her ability, and breathed no word of the ugly sheep-stealing insinuations. How could she send her father and mother away with more worries? She was in bed, but not asleep, when her father returned from Glenisla, and she called to him when he reached the landing.

"Aye, your Granny and Grandfather will be down in the

morning Elspeth," he said, in answer to her query. "They'll try to be here before we leave."

Next morning, at the appointed time, a waggonette arrived from Alyth for Mr and Mrs MacLaine, and at the same time, Elspeth's grandparents arrived. So, with a flurry of goodbyes and good wishes the travellers were off.

This was the first time Elspeth had ever been parted from her mother, and during the first day she had to fight continually against a desire to burst into tears. But her normal good spirits had, in some measure, returned by the following morning, and she went briskly about her duties, determined to take as much responsibility as possible off her grandparents' shoulders.

Rory came over to The Shieling on the second evening to see what had happened to Elspeth and he promised to come as often as possible to keep her up to date with her lessons. As Elspeth accompanied him part of the way home she broached the subject of the sheep stealing rumours, anxious to hear what his opinion might be.

"Aye," he said, "I've heard what they're saying, Elspeth, but don't worry. Your friends would never think that of your father."

Elspeth was much comforted, and it was only on her way back to The Shieling that she remembered she'd forgotten to ask Rory about his old pet Crumpie.

Since a letter at that time took a long time to reach its destination, Elspeth didn't expect any word from her parents for at least ten days from their arrival. There were no door-to-door deliveries in those days but letters and packages arriving by mail coach in Alyth were sent up by special messenger to the roadside cottage in Kilry which served as a shop and a sort of post office. Alternatively, they were dropped off there by some Glendweller who had picked them up in Alyth along with his own. Elspeth told her grandparents she would ride down to the shop and would attend the dancing class at the school on the way back. So she set off on the pony with Ben running alongside.

She was delighted to find a letter awaiting her. Although it was only a hurried note, which her mother had written immediately on arrival at her old home, it was enough to let Elspeth know that they were both safe and well, and that her grandfather, though very ill, had been able to speak to them. Their journey south had been firstly by coach to Dundee, from there to London by boat, and then by coach again to the country village where the old people lived.

Having read the letter Elspeth felt happier and joined eagerly in the dancing. The Dominie was pleased to see her and expressed sympathy on hearing the news of the family trouble.

"Rory McNeill will be able to keep you in touch with the day-to-day work of the class, Elspeth," he said, "and I shall give him a note of any special study we are doing. If you have some free time for reading you can borrow any book you may want from my library."

Elspeth was very grateful for his considerate treatment, but on the way home she found that some of her schoolfellows had put quite a different interpretation on her parents' sudden departure. They taunted her about her parents having run away, and Elspeth thought at first that one of the bigger boys would pull her from her pony. Ben had other ideas, however, he quickly drove off the offender with a well-timed snarl. Being easier in her mind now, following Rory's kind words, and cheered by the headmaster's attitude, Elspeth was determined not to allow the spitefulness to upset her unduly, and hurried home with the welcome letter to show to her grandparents.

Time did not hang heavily on Elspeth's hands during her parents' absence for there was much work to be done around the croft. Most of the malting and distilling at the bothy was attended to by Mr McNeill and Mr Farquharson as her father had said, but Elspeth and Rory did what they could to help there also. The weather had now become bitterly cold, and one day when Elspeth was coming from the byre, she saw a few snowflakes fluttering down from the leaden grey sky. Soon the air was full of feathery flakes. Her grandfather, standing in the doorway of the house, shook his head solemnly.

"You'd best get the sheep down from Kirkhill and in to one of the fields here, near the rest o' the flock, Elspeth, in case we've to carry feeding to them," said the old man, "I think we're in for a storm."

Without more ado, Elspeth slipped on her heavy winter cloak, took down a shepherd's crook from it's nail on the wall, and, calling to Ben, set off up the track to Kirkhill.

Standing at the gate Elspeth carefully counted the sheep as they passed through and was horrified to find that she was six short of the required number. Repeating the process, she counted again but found she was still six short, and a third count made no difference. What could she do? Finally she decided the wisest plan would be to get the sheep she had into safety, for the swirling snowflakes were now beginning to render the visibility very poor. So with Ben's help, she drove the flock down to The Shieling, and then returned to Kirkhill to report the loss to the Innkeeper.

"There's some of my sheep missing too, Elspeth," he said. "It's my opinion the sheep stealers are on the go again. If this continues we'll all be ruined. Come away, lass, and get a drop o' something to heat you up, for ye look quite blue with the cold."

Elspeth was glad of the hot drink made up for her by the Innkeeper's wife, but she was anxious to see if all was well with the sheep at The Shieling so she stayed only a few minutes. Fortunately, she found the home flock was intact and that in itself was a big relief.

"I won't tell Father when I write," she said to her grandparents. "Mother and he have enough to bother about where they are. But what can I do about the missing sheep Grandpa?"

"If the sheep've been stolen there's no' much any of us can do, Elspeth, but maybe the sheep have just strayed. Ye can have a search when the storm's past. Meantime don't worry yourself about them."

Every night, by the light of the cruisie, Elspeth's Grandmother busied herself with the spinning wheel, and after the outside work was finished, Elspeth either took a turn at the wheel or did some reading. On the night of the tragic discovery of the missing sheep she was particularly anxious to forget her worries in a book and she sped through her chores with all possible haste, glad to close the door and join her grandparents by the fire.

Much later, after she had been in bed for a few hours, Elspeth was awakened by a terrified squawking and cackling coming from the hen house. As she lay wondering what could be the reason for the noise, she remembered that she hadn't bolted the hen house door. It must have blown open!

Jumping out of bed she ran to the window but it was too dark to see, and snow was drifting against the panes. Her teeth chattered with cold as she hastily pulled on some clothes and hurried downstairs to light the stable lantern. At the outside door she was met by a flurry of snow and a cruel icy blast, but she pulled her cloak closer around her and hurried on. Rounding the end of the turnip shed, she saw the cause of all the trouble – a fox was emerging from the hen house door with a hen in its mouth!

Yelling loudly, Elspeth waved the lantern and the fox fled, but it did not drop its prey, and Elspeth found two more hens had been killed. Full of remorse for her carelessness, she bolted the henhouse door and returned to the house where her grandparents, alarmed by all the shouting, met her in the lobby.

"It was all my fault," cried Elspeth, throwing herself into a chair and bursting into tears. "I wanted to finish my book and I forgot to lock the hens in last night. Whatever am I to do – first the sheep, and now this! Mother and Father will think I have failed them, and I did so want to do everything properly."

"There! there!" her grandfather comforted her, "don't worry your head about the hens. Your granny and I have some we're wanting rid of, so you can have them. It was only a mistake, and we all make mistakes occasionally. Ye've rather much to do, Elspeth, that's the trouble. But get away back to your bed, lassie. Ye needna be up for a while yet. And maybe the sheep'll turn up safe and sound, Elspeth, just wait till ye see."

Unfortunately, the sheep didn't turn up, and Elspeth soon learned that Kirkhill wasn't the only place to be visited by the sheep stealers. In fact all their neighbours reported similar losses and, although the Town's Officers in Alyth were informed, and made an effort to trace the sheep, they only drew a blank. It was very worrying for all concerned.

The 'Ghost's' Revenge

The storm, fortunately for all, didn't last long. It was followed by heavy rain and a strong west wind, so the snow had cleared away in about a week, for which the Glen people were thankful. A severe storm, with blocked roads, tended to paralyse their activities and brought them much extra work and worry.

On calling at the shop about three weeks after her parents had left, Elspeth received another letter, which broke the sad news that her grandfather had passed away. Although all his family mourned his loss, her mother said they were glad to see him at rest as there had been no hope of recovery. Mr and Mrs MacLaine had attended the simple funeral in the village churchyard and now planned to travel north the following week.

After such news, Elspeth decided not to attend the dancing class. She felt sad to think she would never see her grandfather again but was cheered by the thought that her parents would soon be back home.

During her father's absence, Elpseth and Rory had occasionally been going with Rory's father and Mr Farquharson, to help with the distilling at the bothy. Now Elspeth was anxious to have everything in order for her father's return. The day before her parents were expected home she and Rory went to the bothy by themselves to tidy up. Together they moved the flagstone in the floor which led to a secret cellar underneath. Here they carefully stowed away all the kegs and when the flagstone had been replaced they sat down for a rest.

"It's a long time since the Exciseman was round this way," remarked Elspeth.

"Aye, it is," Rory agreed. "We'd better hide everything in case he should decide to pay a surprise visit, now that the snow's gone. I'll shove the 'head' and the 'worm' up in their usual place under the thatch, and then that's everything out of sight isn't it, Elspeth?"

"Yes. That's everything," said Elspeth, making a careful check, "and we'd better be getting away home, for I'm sure it must be very late. We've been here for ages." Then Elspeth remembered about Crumpie and asked Rory if they'd still got his old pet at Kilwhin.

"I couldn't really tell you Elspeth. After she was put in with the other sheep she didn't bother with me. My brother Rab's the shepherd so I haven't seen Crumpie since the clipping. Then Father sold some sheep to the MacKerachers, and before that, we had some sheep stolen, so I couldn't say whether we still have Crumpie or not. I was sorry to hear that you'd had sheep stolen, especially when you'd been left in charge, Elspeth. There's one thing though, nobody can point a finger at your father now."

"No. I'm glad of that too, Rory," Elspeth agreed, "but I hate to have to tell Father such bad news when he comes back."

After a last look round they called Ben who was curled up and sleeping in a corner, then, having extinguished the lantern, they locked the door and started for home. It was a starry night but there was no moon, so it wasn't very clear as they crossed the fank and when they reached the dyke Ben raised his head and sniffed the air repeatedly. Then he began to make some low, throaty growls. Elspeth peered rather nervously around her.

"There must be someone about," she whispered. "Listen!" But they could hear nothing more than the normal sounds of the Glen at night.

"Maybe he smelt a fox," said Rory. They decided that that must be the explanation for Ben's strange behaviour, and continued on their way over the hill. Ben was not satisfied, however, and would only walk a little way, then stop and sniff again. With ears pricked up he kept looking back towards the bothy.

"D'you know, I think I saw something move back there, myself," said Elspeth, peering through the gloom.

"Och, you're imagining it," said Rory looking hard in the same direction. Then suddenly he started. "You're right enough, Elspeth. I think I saw somebody on horseback. Let's go back a bit and see. It's maybe my father or Mr Farquharson of Drumedge, but we'd better make certain."

Moving as silently as possible, and cautioning Ben to be quiet, they crept back the way they had come. Hiding behind the dyke at the opposite side of the fank from the bothy, they were just able to make out the forms of two men working at the door of the building.

Evidently the men had managed to force the lock, for, suddenly, the door burst in and they heard someone striking a light.

"It's not my father or Mr Farquharson. That's for sure," said Rory. "They've both got keys."

As Elspeth and Rory watched the movement of the light inside the bothy, they could see that the men were making a thorough search, and Elspeth thankfully remembered how

along the wall. Suddenly he stuck against something with his foot. Bending down, he found it was Elspeth.

"Elspeth! Elspeth! Are you hurt?" he shouted, spluttering and choking from the smoke." Come on, Elspeth! We must get out of here!" Rory tried to pull her up and to his relief she stirred, but seemed to have no strength left. Gathering her up as best he could, he turned again towards the door, but his strength gave out and he sank to his knees.

"Ben!" he called, weakly, and, "Ben!" again, almost frantically, until the terrified animal came to his bidding.

Somehow Ben seemed to understand what was required of him, for he grabbed Elspeth's cloak and tried to pull her to the door, but Elspeth was a dead weight and even the combined efforts of Rory and Ben seemed doomed to failure. They were fighting a losing battle.

Just when Rory felt he could do no more there came the sound of running feet and a man's voice sounded in the doorway. In a few moments Elspeth and Rory were both pulled to safety, and it wasn't a moment too soon, for, with a tremendous crash, the roof finally gave way, sending a shower of sparks in all directions.

It took Rory some minutes to recover and it was with amazement he realised who their rescuer was – none other that Elspeth's father!

"Thanks a lot, Mr MacLaine," he panted, "I really thought we were done for."

"By jove, Rory, I had a few anxious moments myself, I can tell you," said Mr MacLaine, who was doing his best to revive Elspeth. "What on earth happened?"

Rory explained the happenings of the evening, by which time Elspeth had quite recovered and was overjoyed to see her father.

"We didn't expect you until tomorrow evening, Father," she cried happily, "but oh, it's good to have you home again!"

"It seems I'm none to soon, Elspeth. Rory's just been telling me all that's been happening, and you were a foolish girl to go into that burning building. Obviously you've just been stunned by your fall but it could have been a tragedy. You could all have been burned to death if the roof had collapsed on top of you."

"But how did you know to come to the bothy?" asked Elspeth.

"Your Granny told me where you'd gone and I thought I'd be better of a breath of fresh air, so I decided I'd walk up to meet you. I was about halfway when I saw the flames. It looks as if the Ghost has had his revenge on us, but from what Rory has told me, its not the revenge he'd had in mind. We'll manage to get a new thatch on before the worst of the weather comes, and nothing else is lost, thanks to you two. Now, if you're feeling better we'll get away home, for there's nothing more we can do here tonight. I'm beginning to think you must have nine lives, like the cat, Elspeth. You have some narrow escapes!"

Over a hearty supper, Mr and Mrs MacLaine described their journeys and spoke sadly of the old man's illness and subsequent death. They also discussed the exiseman's visit to the bothy, but Elspeth's grandmother had advised her to keep the news about the stolen sheep until the next day. She felt the travellers would be in need of a good night's rest, and what Elspeth had to tell them would not be conducive to sound sleep.

So the MacLaine household went to bed immediately after their meal and it was the next morning that Elspeth told her tale of woe about the stolen sheep and the fox raid on the henhouse. She also told them about the cruel insinuations of her schoolfellows regarding the missing sheep, but ended on the same note as Rory had done. "At least no one can point a finger at you now, Father."

"I don't see why they should have doubted me in the first place, Elspeth," replied her father with a worried frown.

The loss of six sheep was a big blow, but to be considered a thief was much worse. He discussed the matter at some length with his parents as he drove them back up the Glen.

"I've been thinking about it all," said the old man, "and I don't like it. Every one of your neighbours had sheep stolen, Sandy, but your flock went scot free. This time you've been a victim, but ye must bear in mind that when they raided Kirkhill, the thieves hadn't been aware that the sheep were yours. They'd been thinking they belonged to the Innkeeper. So far The Shieling itself has never actually been touched. Well, it seems to me you're either being favoured by the thieves, or they're deliberately trying to cast suspicion on you. Whichever way it is, it's a mighty queer business."

A Night to Remember

Mr MacLaine, along with the McNeills and the Farquharsons, set to work without delay and soon re-thatched the bothy, and it was just as well, for towards the middle of December, wintry weather set in with a vengeance. Heavy falls of snow occured, followed by hard frost, and all the lochs and dams, and even the rivers, were covered with thick coatings of ice.

No headway was made in tracing the source of the sheep-stealing and no fresh thefts were reported. Rory had made sure that his schoolfellows heard about the loss the MacLaines had suffered, but with the perversity of human nature, some chose to consider it a ruse of the MacLaines to cover up their own guilt. Rory dared them to mention the matter to Elspeth, but, though nothing definite was said,

Elspeth was painfully aware of the whisperings that went on around her, and of the fact that many of her schoolfellows avoided her company.

Her father also began to fancy that he sensed a change of attitude towards himself on the part of some of his neighbours, although the McNeills and the Farquharsons remained as loyal as ever. He tried to convince himself that he was imagining the difference in the others, but the idea persisted. Yet, at no time did he speak of it to Mrs MacLaine or Elspeth lest they should worry unnecessarily.

Fortunately for Elspeth, her mind was taken up with a new pastime. Her father and mother had brought skates for her and Rory and with the spell of hard frost they were soon practising on the ice. Sledging down the steep snowclad fields was another sport enjoyed by the young, and the not-so-young, at every opportunity, while curling on the frozen lochs and dams was the main spare-time occupation of the adult male section of the community.

"If the frost holds we're to have a curling match with the Minister's team on Kirkhill dam tomorrow," announced Mr MacLaine, coming into the kitchen one bitterly cold night. "I was speaking to the Dominie out there. He wants me to play in his team. By the way, ladies, the Dominie said Mrs McNeill had asked him to remind you that she expects you down at Kilwhin tonight."

"Oh, we hadn't forgotton, Sandy. We're to be helping Mrs McNeill to make a new dress for the Curler's Ball," replied Mrs MacLaine.

"Well, apparently I'm included in the invitation, but I won't manage. It's tonight I've to see the new tenant of the Blackthorn Inn. I got the message on Wednesday. There won't be much chance of seeing him privately until after closing time, and since he's a stranger to these parts I'd prefer to have a chat and find out a little about him before we have any dealings. In any case, I don't want to be seen hanging around the Blackthorn too long, so I'll go down pretty late. If the McNeills wonder where I am you can just say that I had to go to Alyth and I'll be rather late back. If it turns out as I'm hoping, this outlet may prove useful to the McNeills and the Farquharsons as well, but, in the meantime, the less said the better.

"Oh Sandy!" protested Mrs MacLaine. "Is this never to come to an end! Why run yourself into more commitments? Surely it would be better to be done with this smuggling business altogether than to become further involved. If you land in jail what will become of us all then?"

But Sandy MacLaine had no intention of being drawn into another argument about smuggling, so the subject was allowed to drop.

It was the evening of December 24th but not Christmas Eve. Christmas Day in Scotland at that time was Yule Day – five days after the New Year. As soon as the cows had been milked, Elspeth and her mother wrapped their warm cloaks around them and set out over the moor to Kilwhin. The night was clear and frosty with a maze of stars twinkling overhead, and the ground underfoot as hard as iron. It wasn't very good footing, for the path over the moor was rough and uneven, but the bitter cold kept them moving as smartly as possible. When they began to descend the steep field above Kilwhin however, the going became much worse, for the field shone like glass in the light of the lantern and it was almost impossible to keep on their feet.

"Oh, Elspeth! This is dreadful!" cried Mrs MacLaine, after a nerve-wrecking skid. "If you'd told me it was like this I should certainly never have come."

"Oh come on Mother," said Elspeth encouragingly, "It isn't as bad as all that. Hang on to the dyke at that side, and I'll take your arm at this side."

It was no easy task negotiating the steep, ice-bound field but at last, between terrified screams and uncontrollable giggles, the feat was accomplished. Mrs McNeill had been looking out for them, and was waiting to welcome them at the door of the house.

"Come away in and be getting a heat at the fire, for it's a

cold night, and no mistake," she cried, throwing open the kitchen door. "But where's Sandy? Will he be coming down later?"

"I'm afraid not. Sandy asked me to give you his apologies," Mrs MacLaine explained. "He's gone to Alyth, and he'll be late back."

"Sure, that's too bad, now," said Mrs McNeill. "The menfolk were looking forward to having a game of cards with him."

As soon as Mrs MacLaine and Elspeth had thawed their freezing fingers and doffed their cloaks, all three ladies set to work with scissors and needles and thread. The material was spread out at one end of the long kitchen table, while Mr McNeill, Rab, Lachlan, Rory and Andrew McCall, a neighbouring shepherd, played nap at the other end. All were completely engrossed when suddenly a horse neighed from the direction of the farm road.

Mr McNeill dived for the window. Pulling aside the curtain he peered anxiously out. "The Gauger, I'll warrant!" "Just like him to come this night when I was sure the roads would be impossible for him! By jove he has me, and no mistake, if I don't get those barrels out of sight in a couple of hurries! Look now, Rab and Lachie, I'll away out and keep him speaking as long as I can. You nip through the steading and round to the barn. Shove the barrels in the hidey-hole, but for goodness sake, don't make a noise. It's our only hope."

By this time the clang of horses was sounding on the frozen surface of the road quite near the house, and Mr McNeill seized his cap and made for the front door, while his sons slipped out at the back.

Mrs McNeill and Rory made haste to conceal the whisky jar which was kept in the kitchen dresser, while Andrew the shepherd, and Elspeth and her mother tried to appear natural and at ease. There was dead silence while they strained their ears to hear how things were going outside. Little could be gleaned from the voices however, so Mrs McNeill put more logs on the fire and lifted the heavy kettle on to the sway bar.

Suddenly the door was thrown open and a voice was heard singing, "the De'il's awa', the De'il's awa', the De'il's awa' wi' the Exciseman!" It was none other than the Dominie, who, accompanied by the Minister, now danced into the room.

Relief was apparent on every face, and more especially on that of Mr McNeill who had followed the new arrivals into the kitchen.

"By the powers, ye gave me a fright if ever I got one," he said. "Ye'll need to bring the school bell with ye, Dominie, and give us a warning next time ye decide to pay us a late call."

"Well, you see, the lady of the house gave me a message to pass on to Sandy MacLaine this afternoon," laughed the Dominie, "so I thought there would be no harm if the Minister and I joined in the party."

"Sure, there's no harm at all," agreed Mrs McNeill, smiling broadly. "Sit ye inbye to the fire, the pair of ye, and I'll be getting ye all a bite to eat."

"Where's Sandy?" inquired the Minister, looking round the room.

"Unfortunately Sandy couldn't come. He had to go to Alyth." said Mrs MacLaine.

"Could it have been him we saw droving some sheep to Alyth earlier in the evening? I felt sure it was Sandy but the man didn't answer when I called to him and I wasn't so sure then, for Sandy's always ready with a greeting."

"It couldn't have been Sandy you saw. He doesn't have any sheep going to the market tomorrow," said Mrs MacLaine.

"Whereabouts did ye see the sheep?" interrupted Andrew the Shepherd.

"They just turned off on to the hill track below Incheoch as we rode up the main road."

"Its a pity ye didn't make sure who the drover was Minister, considering all the sheep stealing that's going on," remarked the shepherd.

For a moment there was an awkward silence, and Elspeth and Rory's eyes met. Without hesitation Rory rushed into the breach.

"It would be the shepherd from Ravernie," he said. "I heard him telling you he was taking sheep to Alyth, Father."

Mr McNeill seemed slightly surprised by this sudden outburst from his youngest son, but answered evenly enough. "I believe you're right, Rory. He did say something to that effect. It's likely the sheep were Ravernie's, Andra."

The shepherd seemed about to say more, but at this point Mrs McNeill announced that the supper was ready, and the excellence of her bannocks and homemade cheese became the main subject of conversation.

After the meal, Elspeth helped Mrs McNeill to wash up and then Mrs MacLaine said they must be going home.

"Is Sandy coming to meet you?" the Minister inquired.

"I'm afraid not. He expected to be very late back from Alyth."

"In that case, I'll accompany you myself," said the Reverend Gentleman, rising from his seat by the fire. "It's time I was away home anyway."

So the company broke up, with much good-natured teasing about the probable outcome of the forthcoming curling match.

In the meantime, Sandy MacLaine had ridden down to the Blackthorn Inn as requested, and on arrival he found the place ablaze with light. Anxious to make his approach as inconspicuous as possible, he rode into the shadow of some trees at the back of the building and tied his horse there while he scouted around to see how the land lay.

A few horses were tethered near the back door of the Inn and men's voices could be heard coming from an open window at the side of the building so Sandy decided to keep within the shadow of the trees until the coast was clear.

After a time the owners of the horses emerged, strapped what looked like empty whisky kegs to their saddles and after a prolonged conversation with the man whom Sandy took to be the landlord, they rode off. The landlord, then returned to the Inn and closed and barred the door. The lights were then extinguished in every room except that from which Sandy had originally heard the voices coming.

Instinctively he felt that there was something about the atmosphere of the place which warned him to stay away, but having come so far, and waited so long, he was loathe to return home without finding out why the Innkeeper had requested him to call in the first place. Accordingly, he crossed and rapped loudly on the door with his closed fist.

Shuffling feet sounded on the other side of the door and the bolts were withdrawn. Then a very aged head appeared demanding to know who wanted admission at such an hour.

Sandy didn't give his name, but explained that he had business with the landlord, and after looking him over from head to toe in a very insolent manner the old man bade him step inside. Once again the door was carefully barred, Sandy was told to wait where he was, and the old man shuffled off along the passage.

Sandy MacLaine was left in total darkness. He could hear a whispered conversation taking place round a bend further along the passageway, and a few minutes later, the man whom he had previously taken to be the Innkeeper appeared carrying a candle.

"Ye want to see me?" he barked. "Come this way then." Without waiting for an answer, he turned and led the way towards a thin pencil of light which showed underneath a doorway at the far end of the passage.

"Through here," said the Innkeeper, opening the door.

Coming from the darkness of the passage into the light of the room dazzled Mr MacLaine. He was aware of several men talking together but the conversation came to an abrupt halt as he entered, and none of faces that he could make out seemed familiar. No one spoke, and the Innkeeper led the way across the room and out at another door which opened into a sort of entrance hall. Here the man stopped, and placed the candle carefully on a shelf so that the light from it shone full on Mr MacLaine's face, leaving his own in shadow.

"Now," he said, "what's yer business with me?"

"I'm Sandy MacLaine, and I've come in answer to your message," replied Mr MacLaine, eyeing the Innkeeper warily.

"Sandy MacLaine? I never heard of ye before," said the man rudely. "The message couldn't have come from me."

"The messge came from the landlord of the Blackthorn Inn. That's you, isn't it?"

"Aye, I'm the landlord right enough, but I sent no message to you. And I'm not one of them that wants dealings with smugglers either, though I'm led to believe this part of the country is full of them. No doubt ye've a hand in the smuggling business yourself, Mister?" he inquired impudently, peering slyly at Sandy MacLaine from out of the corner of his beady eyes.

Sandy felt his temper rising.

"I didn't come here to discuss my personal affairs with you or anyone else?" he said. "I came because I was told you wanted to see me, and I'd be obliged if you'd come straight to the point and tell me what you wanted to see me about."

"I'm thinking ye've been the victim of a hoax, and I'm real sorry if ye've had a long journey for nothing, Mister," said the Innkeeper, with a harsh laugh.

Sandy waited for no more. He strode across to the door, pulled back the bolt, and let himself out.

As he crossed the yard the Innkeeper's evil laughter echoed in his ears, and anger mounted in him at the thought of the mean trick that had been played on him.

On the long weary ride home he thought of all that had happened at the Blackthorn, and the more he thought about it the more uneasy he became. What purpose did the Innkeeper have in leading him through that lighted room, as if he deliberately wanted him to be seen by all the occupants? If the man had nothing to discuss with him why didn't he tell him so at the back door? There was some ulterior motive behind it all, he felt sure of that. But what? By the time he reached The Shieling he was no nearer an answer.

Mrs MacLaine and Elspeth had long since gone to bed, but the kettle was boiling on the sway, so Sandy made himself a hot drink. He stared thoughtfully into the fire as he drank the steaming liquid. "I'm not likely to forget December 24th for a long time," he said to himself ruefully.

Little did he realise how true those words were to prove!

Brief Encounter

Next morning, as Elspeth and her mother emerged from the byre, the wintry sun was beginning to cast a rosy glow over the eastern sky. There had been quite a heavy fall of snow before daybreak and there was every appearance of more to come.

"A red sky in the morning is the shepherds' warning," quoted Elspeth, pausing to admire the snowy landscape. In the distance she could see her father's tall figure approaching from the direction of Kirkhill and something about the urgency of his walk made her set down her milking pail and wait for him to draw near.

"Is there something wrong, Father?" she called to him.

"Aye, Elspeth, there is. The sheep-stealers have been back at Kirkhill. We've six more sheep missing, and your pet

Daisy's amongst them. The Innkeeper has some missing from his lot as well.''

Elspeth was stunned by the news, and although Mrs MacLaine had breakfast ready, no one had much appetite. Before the meal was over a figure passed the kitchen window and Mr McNeill's voice sounded at the door.

"Are ye there, Sandy?"

"Aye, come in, Tom."

There was no need to ask what was wrong. It was obvious from the worried look on Mr McNeill's face.

"We've lost more sheep," he said, "but worse than that my prize ram's gone!"

"Surely not!" exclaimed Elspeth's father.

"Aye, it is, and Geordie Farquharson has lost his best ram as well."

"That's awful news, Tom. I've some sheep missing from Kirkhill and so has the Innkeeper."

"Well, Geordie Farquharson and Jock Brodie and me are organising a full-scale search. Will you join us Sandy?" asked Mr McNeill turning back towards the door.

"Certainly I will," said Mr MacLaine, following him out.

Elspeth could see, through the little window on to the moor, that most of the neighbouring crofters and farmers had gathered for the search, and she and her mother went out to see what was happening.

"I'll come with you, Rory," Elspeth offered.

"No, Elspeth. There'll be plenty without you this time," interrupted her father. "I was going down to the shop this forenoon to see if any letters had been left there. Your mother is anxious for word from your granny so I think it would be better if you went to the shop instead."

"You could just go down to the shop with Elspeth then, Rory," said Mr McNeill. "Your mother's hoping there'll maybe be a letter from Ireland for her."

"Take the ponies Elspeth. They could do with an airing," her father added as an afterthought.

When the men had left, Elspeth made haste to get ready

for the ride down the Glen, changing quickly into her breeches and leggings as the most suitable attire for the journey. Rory had saddled the ponies, so in no time they were off, for the animals were eager to go.

The gallop over the moor was certainly exhilarating in the wintry sunshine, and Elspeth and Rory had regained their usual good spirits by the time they had reached the cottage shop at the Standing Stone.

"There's been no mail handed in here today," said the lady at the shop. "I doubt they must have had a lot of snow further south."

"Come on, Rory, we'll ride down to Alyth and see if anything has arrived there," suggested Elspeth. "I'll race you to the top of the brae." Away they went, the ponies enjoying the exercise as much as the young people themselves.

"Your mother'll be worried about us, Elspeth," remarked Rory.

"Oh well, it can't be helped," replied Elspeth, "after all, it's for Mother's sake we're doing this. Besides, we shouldn't be long, Rory. The ponies are fresh, and we needn't hinder in Alyth. I heard Mother saying she'd make the dinner later because of the search. Oh, I do hope they find all the missing sheep, Rory," she added wistfully.

They made good time to Alyth and found the little market town extremely busy, mostly with country people stocking up with extra provisions in case of a storm. A mail coach had just arrived and the narrow main street was quite congested.

"If you hold the ponies I'll go and ask about the mail, Elspeth," Rory offered. "Look, if you stand in that close, there, you'll be out of the worst of the traffic."

So they rode into the side opening and Elspeth took charge of Rory's pony while he went off to find out if there were any letters for them. Among the passers-by that jostled with each other near where she sat on her pony, Elspeth saw scarcely a face she recognised, until quite by chance her eye was caught by something familiar in a man's profile. The man had stopped in the street and was talking to another two men, one of whom also struck Elspeth as familiar. She was trying to make up her mind where she had seen the two men before when the first man suddenly turned his full face towards her and she gave a gasp of surprise and recognition.

It was Leo Cleeve! The difference in him was caused by the heavy moustache he had grown. Cleeve seemed to recognise her at the same moment for he gave a start which prompted his companions to turn and look at her also. One was a complete stranger and she didn't like the look of him – but the other she recognised at once. It was the tall dark man of her previous encounters – the man who had rescued her from the river. Elspeth was in the act of raising her hand in acknowledgement when the three men turned, with one accord, and vanished into the crowd as if unwilling to be seen in each other's company.

Elspeth was decidedly shaken by the incident. She couldn't rid her mind of the guilty look which had crossed Leo Cleeve's pale, expressive face when he had seen her looking at him, nor could she forget the speed with which the trio had dispersed into the crowd.

Involuntarily Elspeth shivered, and there flashed through her mind the words of Blind Betsy – "I see three dark strangers!"

"Hi! Elspeth! Are you sleeping?" came Rory's voice beside her and he gave her foot a jerk in the stirrup. "I've spoken to you twice, and you've just sat there and stared in front of you as if you'd seen a ghost!"

It was a relief to hear Rory's teasing tones.

"I'm sorry Rory. What were you saying?"

"I was saying, there's five packages for the Glen and one's for your family and one's for mine," said Rory as he climbed into the saddle. "I have them all in this leather bag and I'll keep them there till we get to Kilry. But what were you staring at, Elspeth?"

"I wasn't staring at anything by that time, Rory, but I got a shock just a wee while before that," and she told him of the reappearance of Leo Cleeve, and of his companions.

"I understood Leo was away back down South," said Rory, "but of course this is the English Christmas holiday time."

"So it is," said Elspeth, "I'd forgotten." But though Rory and she chatted about various matters on their way back to Kilry, the uneasy feeling of approaching calamity persisted at the back of her mind.

It was almost three o'clock before they reached The Shieling and Mrs MacLaine didn't seem sure whether she should be pleased to see them safely home, or angry at their prolonged delay.

"Where have you been all this time? I've been quite worried about you," she scolded them. "And your dinner will be all out of season!"

"We rode down to Alyth for the mail, mother, and if we hadn't done that there would have been nothing at all for you. Whereas, there is this pretty thing," and Elspeth waved the package in front of her mother's face.

"In that case, I shall have to forgive you," smiled Mrs MacLaine, "but don't blame me if your dinner isn't as good as usual."

"Have they found any trace of the sheep?" Elspeth inquired as soon as they were seated at the table.

"No. Your father was here about an hour ago but there were no developments at that time. The men have gone to make inquires somewhere else. It's all very worrying."

When they had eaten their fill, Elspeth and Rory helped with the washing up. Then they set off with Elspeth's sledge, to have a run down one of the steep fields. When darkness began to fall they returned to the house, as there were the usual outdoor jobs to be done, including those normally undertaken by Mr MacLaine. Rory lent a hand with everything, and when they had finished, Mrs MacLaine called them to come and have a bite to eat. There was still no sign of the searchers and it was a rather silent trio which sat round the table in the flickering firelight.

"I'd better be getting back, in case Mother's still on her

own," said Rory at last, so Elspeth, as usual, accompanied him part of the way home. When she returned, her mother was already busy at her spinning wheel, so Elspeth sat down to do some knitting, but at the first sound of her father's heavy boots on the flagstones outside, Elspeth was at the door.

"Any luck, Father?" she inquired anxiously.

"No luck, Elspeth," he said wearily, as he closed the outside door and hung up his crook. "We've had a hard day, haven't we Ben?" Mr MacLaine bent to give the collie's head a pat before slumping into his chair by the fire.

"You must be hungry, Sandy," said Mrs MacLaine, full of concern at the sight of her husband's haggard face and drooping shoulders.

"No, I'm not hungry Mary. We had a bite of supper from Mrs Farquharson. I'm just tired with tramping through the snow all day, and of course I'm worried – we all are."

Then Elspeth told her father about her brief encounter with Leo Cleeve in Alyth, and of how the men seemed anxious to get out of her sight.

"Well now Elspeth, you could hardly expect Cleeve to be delighted to see you after what we did to him that night at Kirkhill, but if he's on the go again, we'd better be keeping a closer lookout for Willie McDougall's washing line. I'm not as worried about the Gauger as I am about this sheep stealing business though. Those men are really cunning. We certainly got on the move quick enough this time but we didn't find a trace. Of course that heavy snowfall in the early morning completely obliterated all footprints. We were really unlucky there. However, young Rab McNeill went off to Alyth to notify the Town's Officers so we'll just have to see what they can make of it.

"The Minister and the Dominie must have been disappointed about their curling match," remarked Mrs MacLaine.

"Aye, they were that, but of course it was impossible, and we haven't made any future plans in that direction either. Nobody has much heart for games at the moment."

A Chapter of Calamities

The next day being Sunday, nothing was done about the missing sheep. Owing to the very bad walking conditions the MacLaine household didn't go to church either, and since no form of sport was countenanced on the Sabbath day, Elspeth couldn't take out her sledge. So most of the day was spent in reading, and by bedtime Elspeth was even tired of her book and was quite glad to make her way up the ladder to bed, even though she didn't feel much like sleeping. Actually, Elspeth was dreading the next day at school, for the fresh outbreak of the sheep stealing would no doubt bring more taunts and thinly veiled accusations from some of her school-fellows.

The early forenoon saw the arrival in the Glen of the Town's Officers. Having received all the necessary information regarding the missing sheep, the Officers made a systematic tour of the various homesteads, questioning the inhabitants about their activities on the night of December 24th, when the sheep had gone missing.

Sandy MacLaine had been dreading this questioning for he knew it would be difficult to explain away his visit to the Blackthorn Inn. However, he could do nothing more than tell the truth, and after all, he had nothing to hide as regards the sheep. So he told the Officers that he had made a very brief call at the Inn, and that the Innkeeper would no doubt corroborate his statement since he had talked with him personally.

Fortunately the senior of the two officers was acquainted with Sandy MacLaine and knew him to be an honest man, so he accepted the statement. He made a note of it in his book and gave the order to proceed to the next house on their list.

Elspeth's father heaved a sigh of relief but he wasn't entirely surprised when the Officers appeared again at The Shieling the following day.

"The Landlord of The Blackthorn says he has never even heard of a Sandy MacLaine, far less spoken to him," said the Town's Officer apologetically, "I'm afraid you'll have to accompany us to the Inn."

As he saddled his pony, Sandy MacLaine was filled with a nameless dread. How on earth could he prove that he had been at the Inn if the Innkeeper persisted in denying his visit? Mrs MacLaine was extremely worried also as she saw her husband leave with the Officers. She instinctively felt that there was dirty work afoot.

To make matters worse, the men had hardly left when a messenger came from Glenisla to say that old Mrs MacLaine, Elspeth's grandmother, had been taken ill. Obviously the old man would never manage to cope alone, so Mrs MacLaine decided at once that Elspeth must go to their aid. She asked the messenger if he would continue down to the school and fetch Elspeth.

Mrs MacLaine had everything ready for Elspeth when they returned.

"I'm sorry you'll have to stay off school again Elspeth," she said, "but you'll be on holiday on Friday anyway, so it'll only be for a few days, and we may be able to make other arrangements by the weekend."

"I don't mind, Mother. I'll enjoy looking after Gran, and I love hearing Grandfather's tales about old times in the Glen," said Elspeth cheerfully as they ate a hasty meal.

Ben showed a great desire to go with Elspeth and Mrs MacLaine agreed, as there wasn't so much work to be done amongst the sheep at that time of year, and she knew Elspeth would be happy to have the dog's company.

To Elspeth's queries regarding where her father was, Mrs MacLaine merely replied that he had gone to Alyth and would be back at any moment, so it didn't occur to Elspeth that there was anything amiss. She bade her mother a cheerful goodbye, promising to let her know how the invalid progressed, and the travellers made haste to be off, for they were anxious to be at their destination before darkness fell. Had Elspeth known what was happening at the Blackthorn Inn, however, she would not have proceeded up the Glen so light of heart.

When Sandy MacLaine and his escort had dismounted at the Inn the landlord had come to the door and the Senior Officer asked if Mr MacLaine was familiar to him.

With an absolutely blank expression, the Innkeeper looked Sandy over and then a flicker of recognition showed in his face.

"By Jove! Now, he is familiar to me!" he exclaimed. "He's the shepherd from the Glen that sometimes stops here for a night while his sheep are resting on the market muir. He was here at the end of the week, I believe, but I didn't see him myself. It was Jamie that attended to him. Hey, Jamie!" he called, and the old man who had admitted Sandy on the night of his appointment with the Innkeeper, immediately shuffled out from where he had obviously been eavesdropping behind the door.

"You know this shepherd do ye not, Jamie?" the Innkeeper asked.

"Aye, I know him right enough," answered the old man, screwing up his wizened face as he eyed Mr MacLaine with his bleary old eyes. "He came here late on Friday night. Hadn't been here for a while before that."

"What have you to say to this, MacLaine," demanded the officer, turning to Sandy.

"What can I say? What can anybody do with a liar?" answered Sandy choking back his rage as he realised the plot that was being hatched against him. "It's all a fabrication of lies, you must see that."

At this point another man appeared in the doorway and the Innkeeper turned to address the newcomer, "Good lad, Jeck, ye've just come at the right time," he said. "You're the very man we need. This man says we're telling lies about him, but take a good look at him and tell me if ye haven't seen him two or three times at this Inn on his way to the markets at Blair, and Coupar Angus, and Perth?"

The man stroked his chin and looked insolently at Mr MacLaine.

"Aye! I have that," he answered. "He had some fine sheep too, the other night – two grand rams. I could have done fine with them myself."

The Town's Officer gave a start at the mention of the rams, and Sandy MacLaine took a step forward, his hands clenched and fury in his eyes, but the Officer held him back. Turning to his fellow officer, he indicated Sandy and said, "take charge of this man." To the other three he said, "come inside, I want to talk to you."

When he emerged from the Inn a short time later, the Officer's face was very grave. He said nothing, but signed to Sandy MacLaine and the other officer to remount, and they moved off at once.

"I'm sorry, MacLaine," he said after a bit, "but you'll need to go to Alyth with us. This has turned out a much more complicated matter than I expected. Between you and me, I think you're up against it. Not that I fancy that gang myself, but they have their story, and they intend to stick to it."

"But surely you don't believe them!" expostulated Sandy MacLaine. "I'm telling you the truth when I say I never spent an hour in that place in my life. The first time I crossed the doorstep was on Friday last, in answer to a message the landlord sent to me. When I arrived he denied point blank ever asking me to come, so I only stayed about ten minutes with him. If you ask me, that crowd's using me for their own ends, but how I should be their victim is more than I know. They're all strangers to me."

"Quite so," replied the Officer, "and if I know their type, it'll be a difficult job to turn the tables on them. In the meantime I'm afraid we'll have to detain you."

"You mean I'm under arrest!" gasped Sandy MacLaine. "Surely you wouldn't arrest me on the evidence of men like that!"

"It's not entirely on their evidence," said the officer ruefully, "Several Kilry people hinted that you were connected in some way with the sheep-stealing."

"Surely not! What possible reason could they have for saying such a thing? I've never stolen anything in my life. And how am I to get word to The Shieling that you're holding me here? My wife will be worried about me if I don't get home before dark."

"We'll get word to her," replied the Officer, and Sandy could see that any further argument on his part would be quite useless.

Elspeth, of course, knew nothing of all this, and once at her grandparents' home she cheerfully set to work to get the household chores under control and to make her grandmother as comfortable as possible.

On the day following her arrival, a letter was delivered to old Mr MacLaine and Elspeth could see that the old man was greatly put out by the contents. He passed no remark to her, although every now and again he opened the letter and perused the contents with an exceedingly worried air. That evening a blizzard came to the Glen and the next day the roads were completely blocked, but a thaw set in almost at once, and with a west wind blowing up, the snow soon began to show signs of melting.

Just after mid-day on the 31st December Elspeth saw her grandfather get out his quill pen and writing materials, and set to work to pen a fairly lengthy epistle which he read and re-read before he seemed quite satisfied with the wording.

"I'd like you to walk up to the Manse and deliver this letter to the Minister, Elspeth," he said. "See that you give it to no one but him. I'll borrow your pony and ride down the Glen a wee bit. I want a word with Willie McDougall."

Quite pleased at the idea of getting out for a walk, Elspeth set off very willingly with Ben bounding in front.

"I'm sorry, Elspeth, the Minister's not at home," said Mrs McAllister the housekeeper, "but he shouldn't be long. Come away in. I was just about to make a cup of tea so you can drink a cup with the Minister," and she showed Elspeth into the Minister's study.

Elspeth was warming her hands at the fire when she was startled by a cry from the housekeeper, "Elspeth! Elspeth! Come quickly!" and dashing along the passage in the direction from which the voice came, she found the poor woman struggling to lift the Minister who had slipped and fallen at the back door, injuring his right leg.

Between them, Elspeth and the housekeeper succeeded in getting the reverend gentleman into a chair in the kitchen but it was obvious that his leg was badly hurt, for the man was in great pain.

Having got him seated, the housekeeper fetched a little brandy which revived him considerably. He was able to explain that he had fallen while hurrying across from the Inn. "I had just heard, from a reliable source, that the excisemen were on their way down from Drumore in full strength, accompanied by troopers," he said. "They're planning a full-scale raid on the smuggling fraternity by moonlight. Obviously their idea is to catch the smugglers when they're off guard, making merry and celebrating Hogmanay. A particularly mean trick, if I may say so."

Then Elspeth remembered her grandfather's letter, and the Minister opened it at once.

"Good gracious, Elspeth," he exclaimed, "this is serious news, and doubly so when this excise raid is about to take place and your father not at home."

"My father not at home!" gasped Elspeth. "But where is he then?"

"You don't know anything about the message contained in this letter Elspeth?" the Minister asked.

"No I don't," replied Elspeth.

The Minister hesitated, looked at the letter again, then cleared his throat. "If your mother had thought it necessary for you to know, she would have told you, so we'll just leave it at that in the meantime."

"Is my father ill?" Elspeth asked anxiously.

"No, no it's nothing to do with his health. He has been unexpectedly called away, that's all. I shall be writing an answer to your grandfather's letter, but first of all I must think of a way of warning the smugglers of what is about to descend upon them. We can't just sit here doing nothing while the excisemen ransack the Glen."

The Minister tried to raise himself from the chair, but at the merest pressure on his leg he cried out with agony, and in spite of this new worry of her own, Elspeth realised that something would have to be done about his leg, and also about the excise raid. It was obvious the Minister was unable to move from the house.

"I'll go over the hill and warn the people in Kilry," she offered.

"But you can't go yourself, Elspeth. It will soon be dark," the Minister pointed out.

"Oh, I could find my way blindfolded, and I'm not afraid in the dark."

"Do you have your pony?"

"No. My Grandfather has the pony, but I could easily walk over the hill. I have Ben for company."

"You could have had my pony," said the Minister, "but she cast a shoe this morning."

"I think I'd be better on foot than with a strange horse," said Elspeth. "The only snag is, I have my grandmother in bed so I have her to think about. I can hardly go off and leave her."

"I'll go down and attend to your granny as soon as I have this man safely in bed," offered Mrs McAllister. "You might run over to the Inn and get someone to come and help us, Elspeth."

The Innkeeper himself came back with Elspeth to help the Minister into bed.

"I'll send the stable-boy to fetch the Doctor from Alyth," he said. "He can go down by Dykends and Bellaty and warn the folk on the East side o' the Glen."

"That'll be a great load off my mind," said the Minister. "Elspeth has offered to walk over the hill to Kirkhill Inn and they'll let the Kilry folk know from there. You'll need to give Elspeth a dish of tea and something to eat before she starts," he added, turning to his housekeeper.

"Aye. I have it ready, and I'm thinking she'll need it to heat her up before she goes out on that hill this night. I'm sure it's to be frost yet," said the housekeeper. "Now don't you worry about your Granny, lass. I'll go down and see the old couple right away."

So Elspeth ate and drank what Mrs McAllister had prepared for her. Then she and Ben set out at once on their journey over the hill to Kilry.

Ben Sees it Through

It was a bitterly cold afternoon showing signs of early
darkness as Elspeth and Ben crossed the footbridge over the
Isla and breasted the hill. The snow was deep and difficult to
walk amongst, and before they had proceeded far, a freezing
fog had wrapped them around like a thick icy blanket. It was
as if they were in a world of their own, and indeed Elspeth felt
very much alone, in spite of Ben's company. The ghostly
shapes of trees looming up through the mist were quite
frightening to Elspeth, and even made Ben growl uncertainly,
while the depth of the snow in parts made it impossible to
keep to any definite direction. Elspeth stumbled into a hill
burn occasionally, and sometimes into a marshy peat bog.
After several plunges into deep drifts her hands and feet
were numbed with cold and wet. Soon she realised she was

completely lost. She stopped and tried to work out the direction in which she should be going but found she simply had no idea which was the right way, and the Kirk Road was non-existent in that snowy waste. The only hope was to keep moving until they came on some familiar landmark.

Having plodded on for what seemed like hours, Elspeth suddenly fancied she saw a light in the distance. The thought that perhaps it might be coming from Kirkhill spurred her on to greater efforts but sadly the light, if indeed there had ever been a light, vanished, and Elspeth shivered at the memory of tales she had heard of the treacherous Will o' the Wisp luring travellers to their doom. After some time a tiny pinpoint of light again appeared through the fog and this time it seemed to remain stationary, so Elspeth decided to head for it as a last hope. Although it had at first seemed fairly near she found that it was, in fact, quite a distance away, but she struggled on through the snow, and on closer scrutiny, she was thankful to see that the light was definitely coming from a building. To her disappointment as she approached the building she realised that it was certainly not Kirkhill, nor was it like any place she had ever seen before. Looming out of the mist it became apparent that it was a tumbledown ruin, but the bleating of sheep from the fank beside the building informed her that a flock of sheep was gathered there.

The light came from a small deep-set window and some strange instinct prompted Elspeth to peep through the window before she approached the door. Stealthily she crossed and looked inside. As she did so her heart missed a beat for it was no ordinary scene that met her eyes. The room contained three occupants – one was Leo Cleeve, the other was Angus MacKeracher, the man who had rescued her from the river, and the third she recognised as the man who had made up the trio on that brief encounter in Alyth. They were three evil-looking men as they sat together engrossed in a card game, and it was obvious, even to Elspeth's inexperienced eye, that it wasn't just a friendly game. The men were gambling, and by the piles of gold and silver pieces it was apparent they were playing for heavy stakes. They were all drinking heavily, and the angry voices and foul language proved that they were in disagreement.

Elspeth literally began to shake with fright. She felt sure these men must be connected in some way with the Exciseman's raid. After all, Leo Cleeve and the exciseman had been hand-in-glove with each other. If they were to find her here now all would be lost! She must get to Kilry before them!

Moving as quickly and as silently as possible, Elspeth hurried round the corner of the house seeking to find some path leading away from the place. Unfortunately, as she hastened along, she stumbled against the corner of an old shed and dogs within the shed began to bark excitedly. Elspeth called Ben to her, and, keeping a hold on him she dashed behind the high wall of the sheep fank and threw herself on her face, pulling the collie down beside her.

She was none too soon, for the door of the house was thrown open violently and the men came lumbering out, one of them holding the lantern aloft.

"I tell you, I heard something," came the voice of Leo Cleeve in an argumentative tone.

"A piece of nonsense," returned MacKeracher irritably. "There's not a sound, except those blasted dogs. Shut up will ye," he yelled at the dogs, aiming a kick at the door of the shed.

"Och, he just wanted to capsize the table and get the money mixed up," roared the third man. "Who could be roaming around this god-forsaken place on a night like this!"

"Certainly not Sandy MacLaine, anyway," remarked MacKeracher, with a sinister laugh.

"Why Sandy MacLaine in particular?" asked Cleeve.

"Ha! Ha! Ha!" roared MacKeracher. "Because Sandy MacLaine's deputising for us in Alyth jail at the moment, that's why."

"In Alyth jail?" queried Cleeve in an astounded voice.

"Aye! In Alyth jail. He was arrested on Tuesday for sheep-stealing, thanks to me," claimed the third man, thumping his chest with evident pride. "My little plan worked, ye see, and it's one hundred per cent foolproof. I saw to that. Come on and let's finish the game, you lads. The moon's coming through the mist, and we'll need to be on our way ere long. The frost's gripping hard, so that'll be a benefit." With that, the men returned to the house, slamming the door behind them.

Elspeth was stunned by the import of this brief conversation. Jail! Jail! Jail! The word seemed to hammer itself into her mind! Her father was in jail – arrested for stealing the sheep that those men had stolen! The Minister had said he was away from home, but never for one moment had she imagined anything like this. Fresh terror took hold of Elspeth at this point, for the desperateness of her own position struck her with renewed force. If those men were to discover her now they would have no mercy for they would guess that she had overheard what they had said, and conviction of sheep-stealing meant the supreme penalty. The supreme penalty! Then her father could go to the gallows for a crime he had never committed! Blind Betsy had spoken the truth! "I see the shadow of the gallows," she had said.

The bleating of a sheep in the fank beside her spurred Elspeth into action. Those sheep were stolen sheep, she knew that now, beyond a doubt, and there was only one course of action open to her. Whatever happened, she must get the sheep out of the fank and take them with her before those men could stop her. It was the only way to prove her father's innocence.

The sheep were lying, or standing, ruminating contentedly, and, as she looked at them, Elspeth gave a start, for there, quite near her, she was sure she saw Daisy, her pet lamb. It was on the tip of her tongue to call out her pet's name, but she remembered that the dogs would hear her and would, undoubtedly start barking again at the strange voice. Better to try to draw her pet's attention without frightening all the sheep.

As the moon penetrated the mist, Elspeth could see around her more distinctly, and she now recognised the tumbledown place as a disused croft which her father had pointed out to her when they were looking for the lost sheep in the Autumn. What was it he had called it, again? The Auld Biggin? Yes, that was the name. Once she had the sheep away from here she would soon work out the direction of the homeward path.

Ben had meanwhile been sniffing around beside her and the sheep had drawn closer out of curiosity. Daisy was amongst those nearest to Elspeth, so she whispered her pet's name in an undertone and held out her hand. The lamb hesitated a moment, sniffed uncertainly, then, with a deep throaty bleat, she came to Elspeth who hugged her and whispered in her ear. Daisy had provided the answer to the problem. Elspeth would lead her pet out of the fank and take a chance on the rest of the sheep following Daisy.

Alas! Just as she was about to put her plan into action, the door was thrown open again and the figure of one of the men was silhouetted against the light. Elspeth stood rooted to the spot, unable to move, but the man wasn't looking for intruders. He went into the old stable and emerged almost immediately with what appeared to be a bag of money. Then he strode back into the house and Elspeth could hear a heated argument taking place, for he had left the door of the house slightly ajar.

After this latest scare Elspeth felt so weak she thought she wouldn't be able to walk. Her whole body trembled, but she knew the time was now or never. Daisy was still keeping close beside her and Ben was lying at her feet with his nose between his paws. Swiftly Elspeth indicated to Ben to round up the sheep, patting his nose to let him know to be quiet in his work. Then she turned and led the way to where a spar of wood had been fixed across a gap in the wall. She unfixed the spar and stepped out over the dyke. Daisy followed at once, but for a moment Elspeth thought the rest of the sheep were not to follow. Then, as Ben rounded them up, they too dashed for the break in the dyke and came pelting on behind

Elspeth and her pet, as they sped over the snow and up round the back of the cottage.

Surprisingly enough, not a sheep bleated, but the rustle of their heavy fleeces, as they bounded over the dyke, sounded like thunder in Elspeth's ears, and she expected to hear a shout behind her at any moment. Terror seemed to lend wings to her feet and she covered the difficult snow-clad hillside with amazing speed. If only she could get over the brow of the hill before the escape was discovered. Alas! before she had quite topped the rise, angry yells from below warned her that the sheep's disappearance had been discovered.

Luck was on Elspeth's side yet, however, for a bank of cloud drifted across the moon, making the landscape hazy. Just as she reached the summit, though, a shaft of moonlight broke through and by the increase in the yelling, Elspeth knew her flight had been observed.

Suddenly a gunshot broke the stillness of the night and a bullet whistled past, followed by another, and then Elspeth felt an explosion in her arm which seemed to blow it to pieces. She sank to her knees clutching the injured arm. Every thing whirled round, but desperation forced her to get up and stumble on, although she felt very sick and faint. Somewhere behind her she heard another shot and then a weird, blood-curdling yell, and then silence, but Elspeth kept struggling on, with Daisy and the flock hard on her heels and Ben bringing up the rear.

The pain in Elspeth's arm was now almost unbearable and her sleeve was soaked with blood which trickled over her hand and dripped on to the snow. She felt very sick, and her breath was catching in sobs as she stumbled down the hill-side. She dared not think of the distance still to be covered. After falling and struggling to her feet over and over again, she finally felt she couldn't go another step. The sheep were now passing her on their headlong rush downhill, but Daisy kept by her side and Ben too, with tongue lolling out, seemed more inclined to stay with his mistress than continue with the sheep alone.

"Go on! Go on, Ben!" Elspeth urged, half in tears. "Home! Home Ben!" and at last the wise collie seemed to understand and sped off to round up the stragglers and drive the flock faster than ever towards Kirkhill.

Elspeth slowly and painfully trailed behind, accompanied by Daisy, until at last, stumbling into a deep drift, she found she hadn't the strength to raise herself and everything swam into darkness. The last Elspeth knew was of Daisy sniffing at her face and bleating uncertainly beside her.

Meanwhile, Ben drove the sheep at considerable speed, straight to Kirkhill, and Mr McKay, the Innkeeper, surprised to hear the bleating at such a late hour – for it was nearly eight o'clock – opened the door and went to investigate. He was just in time to see the dog drive its charges through an open gateway into a field. Pulling on a coat, the Innkeeper hurried to close the gate while Ben looked up at him with tongue lolling out and tail wagging.

"So it's you, Ben!" exclaimed Mr McKay in amazement. "Good dog, Ben! Good dog!" and he patted Ben's head. "But where did ye get the sheep lad? Where's your master, Ben?"

For answer, Ben looked back up the hillside. Pricking up his ears he looked straight ahead, then gave a yelp and whined a little, and at last he grabbed the old man's coat sleeve and pulled, to show him that he wanted him to come. Then running a little way ahead he repeated the process and returned to pull the Innkeeper's coat sleeve as before.

"Wait till I tell my wife, and get my boots tied and I'll come with ye, lad," said the old man and he hurried back inside while Ben barked his disapproval of the delay. They soon set out again, however, and Ben was so anxious he gave himself double the journey, running on in front and then back again to see if the man was following.

The dog's sureness of purpose inspired the Innkeeper to follow as fast as he could, but it was a considerable distance from the Inn to the spot where Elspeth had fallen and the snowclad slopes proved hard going. The Innkeeper began to wonder if perhaps he had been rather foolhardly in answering the dog's appeal, and when Ben stopped and sniffed the air and began to run uncertainly hither and thither Mr McKay was convinced he'd been mad to come so far.

As he watched he saw that Ben always returned to the same spot, but there appeared to be nothing there. However, having come this far he decided he would continue to that point. All of a sudden a loud bleat rang out and he saw a sheep approach Ben, hesitantly at first, but growing gradually bolder, while the dog wagged its tail and gave obvious signs of recognition.

In the moonlight on that bare hillside, the whole business suddenly appeared decidedly uncanny and unreal to the old man, but when he reached the spot where Ben had stopped, he was quickly jerked out of the feeling of unreality for there, in the snow, was a very real bloodstain. There was also a deep indenture as if someone had fallen heavily, and the snow was churned up by serveral large, and some small footprints.

Involuntarily, the Innkeeper shuddered, and peered nervously around him. Ben had now moved ahead, with the sheep following, and, as the old man stepped forward he could see a trail of bloodstains in the snow. The thought that someone was in need of help spurred him on.

As they proceeded up the hill, the sheep turned occasionally towards the Innkeeper, half deciding to go to him and then giving a loud bleat and scampering after Ben. The old man felt there was something familiar about the sheep but his attention was fully required in the ascent of the hill so he ceased to bother about the strange liaison between the lone sheep and the collie dog. Fully an hour after he had left Kirkhill, Ben led him down to The Auld Biggin.

A Race Against Time

And what, in the meantime, had happened to Elspeth?

When the three men had discovered that the sheep had been taken from the fank, Angus MacKeracher had run for his gun, it was he who had fired the random shot which had struck Elspeth's arm. Then, dashing forward in pursuit of the flock, he had tripped and fallen, the gun having gone off in such a way that he received the full charge in his side. The blood-curdling shriek which Elsepth had heard was the cry he uttered as he fell.

Leo Cleeve and the other man were horror-stricken. A quick examination of their companion showed them that he was quite dead. Cleeve was for carrying him to the house but the other cried, "No! Leave him where he is. Then they'll never know there was more than one at this job."

So they left the dead man where he had fallen and turned back to the house.

"I'm getting out of here," said Cleeve's companion. "There'll be the devil and all to pay. Don't bother about the sheep. Let's get going while the going's good!"

Cleeve's face in the lantern light betrayed the struggle within. Obviously the temptation to run was strong in him also, but still he hesitated.

"No," he said at last. "I've been a mighty big fool to get implicated in all this, but I'm not to be party to a murder, and I think it was just a girl that Angus fired at. Wouldn't be surprised if it was Elspeth MacLaine herself that took the sheep. That shot hit her too, for she fell. I'm going to see if she's lying up there."

"Don't be a fool," bellowed the other. "Bad enough if she was struck, but it'll be worse for us if we're proved to be mixed up in this sheep-stealing business. There's no doubt we'll hang for it. You're crazy if ye bide here. But I'm warning ye, don't bring my name into this if ye're brought to trial!" He turned towards the door but then he stopped as if struck by a sudden thought, and his face was ugly as he turned to face Cleeve again. His eyes had narrowed to mere slits and his chin was thrust forward menacingly.

"By heavens! maybe I'd better put paid to you right now," he snarled. "Then I can be sure ye'll not split on me."

"Why should I implicate you even if I am caught?" returned Cleeve. "It wouldn't help me any. Clear out if you want to clear out. I'm going to see if there's a girl lying hurt over the hill there. If my fears are unfounded I'll soon follow you."

The other man still hesitated as if undecided whether to trust Cleeve or not, then he turned again to his heel and lunged outside and round to the tumbledown stable where he saddled his horse and rode off, slanting along the hillside in a westerly direction rather than taking the direct route by Kirkhill Inn.

Cleeve, meanwhile, made his way as quickly as possible on

foot in the direction taken by Elspeth and the flock of sheep. On reaching the brow of the hill he peered across the snow-covered landscape, but though the moon was high in the sky, visibility on the ground itself was not too good, for shadows from rocks and boulders cast an uneven pattern over the glistening expanse of whiteness. Suddenly, however, his eye was caught by a dark spot in the snow, and stepping forward to examine it he found it to be a bloodstain. Then he saw another and another and so on, until, by the frequency of the spots and the zig-zagging course of the footprints, it was obvious that the victim was fast losing strength.

Cleeve peered in front of him again, and the form of Daisy the sheep became discernible in the distance bending over a dark object in the snow which was, of course, Elspeth. Daisy bleated once or twice and drew back to a safe distance as Cleeve approached and bent to examine the limp, death-like form. Ripping the sleeve of her dress, he examined Elspeth's arm, which was still bleeding profusely, but he decided after a quick inspection that the wound would not be as deadly as the intense cold, for the night was freezing hard.

Quickly he removed the kerchief he wore round his neck and bound up the arm to stop the bleeding, then, picking Elspeth up as gently as possible, he made his way back over the hill to the ruined croft. Daisy followed for a little way but finally returned to the spot where Elspeth had fallen, bleating anxiously now for her companions.

On reaching the old croft, Cleeve laid Elspeth on the rough bed of dried bracken and heather which some previous occupant had piled in a corner beside the fireplace. Then he proceeded to try to rub some heat back into her frozen limbs, and succeeded in forcing a few drops of whisky between her blue lips. Gradually he noted with satisfaction that she was showing signs of recovery. Next he built up the fire to heat the room, and boiled some water in the battered old kettle. Then he set about examining the wounded arm and cleansing it as best he could. Elspeth cried out with pain but she did not seem to recognise Cleeve and called anxiously for her father and mother and Ben, and for Daisy the lamb, until she again lapsed into unconsciousness.

Leo Cleeve looked at her anxiously as he made her as comfortable as possible on the bed of bracken and heather. From the stable he fetched a horse rug and covered her with that, together with his cloak and her own. He knew he must get help as quickly as possible and get her removed to where she could be properly nursed. Should he risk leaving her alone, perhaps for hours, until he found his way to Kirkhill or to Glenisla Inn? Or would he be better to wrap her up and take her with him on the pony? Yet what might be the consequences of such a journey in the bitter cold? It was difficult to know what to do for the best.

He turned back to the patient again and felt her pulse. It was certainly weak, and her face had a deathly pallor. In that dilapidated building, with the moonlight streaming through the holes in the roof and the leaping flames casting grotesque shadows on the rough stone walls, the atmosphere was uncanny, to say the least of it. A shiver ran down Cleeve's spine. All his evil past began to loom up in front of him. Sinking on to a chair beside the table, where only an hour or two ago he and his partners in crime had gambled and quarrelled, he buried his face in his hands and groaned aloud.

He must have dozed, for when he next looked at the fire he found that it had burned low and the room felt cold. Full of concern for Elsepth he hastened to pile on more logs and, as he did so, a frenzied barking broke out amongst the dogs. Someone was coming! His first impulse was to find a hiding place, but even as the thought crossed his mind, a moan from Elspeth held him back. Roused by the barking of the dogs, she was struggling to raise herself, and began to cry, "Where am I? Where am I?" in a weak, bewildered voice.

"It's all right, Elspeth," Cleeve answered. "Don't try to speak now. Lie down and sleep," and he tucked the rough coverings more closely around her. She seemed anxious to say something, but her strength failed. She sank back again and closed her eyes. Leo Cleeve crossed quickly to the window and peered outside.

The furious barking of the dogs in the shed continued. Then he saw another dog sniffing at the shed door and a single sheep came rather hesitantly into his line of vision. There was something familiar about both these animals, and also about the man who was bending over the stiff figure of MacKeracher. Leo looked closer: it was Mr McKay, the Innkeeper at Kirkhill!

Leo Cleeve felt like a rat in a trap. There was no escape now. He must brave the matter out and take the consequences. The Innkeeper was already approaching the house so Cleeve went out to meet him.

"In the name of creation, man! what's been happening here this night?" queried the old Innkeeper in shocked surprise. "Am I seeing right – it is Cleeve, isn't it?"

"Yes. It is Leo Cleeve, I regret to say," was the humble reply. "But how do you happen to be here Mr McKay? It's a fair distance to the Inn from this place."

"That dog," said the old man, indicating Ben with his stick, "led me up here, though how he happened to be around at this time of night is more than I know. He brought a flock of sheep to Kirkhill and then led me back here. What's that he's at now?" Ben started to scratch with both feet at the door of the house.

"By jove! He's certainly a wise dog." cried Cleeve. "He knows Elspeth's in there."

"Elspeth!" exclaimed the Innkeeper. "Surely not!"

"Aye that she is, sir, and very ill too, I'm afraid. She has a gunshot wound in the arm. Come and have a look at her."

Mr McKay followed Cleeve into the house. Ben was at Elspeth's side in a flash and stood with his head on the cover beside hers, whining anxiously and wagging his tail. She opened her eyes as the men approached but it was obvious she didn't recognise either of them and they failed to catch what she was saying.

Even to the Innkeeper's inexperienced eye it was obvious

she was far from well. "We must get a doctor," he said. "Explanations must wait."

"Take a drop of something to revive you," said Cleeve, seeing that the old man was showing signs of fatigue. "I'll go back to Kirkhill, or up to Glenisla for help, if you stay here with Elspeth," and Leo hurried outside to saddle his horse.

With a shaky hand Mr MacKay began to pour himself a drink from the flask which Cleeve had indicated on the table, but he was interrupted by a weak voice from the bed. As swiftly as he could, he crossed to Elspeth's side, and bending close to her, he caught the whispered words. "The Gauger's to raid the Glen by moonlight tonight. I must let them know in Kilry! I must! The Minister said so. Where's Ben? Where's Father? O dear, I'm so tired, and my arm hurts so!" and the last word ended in a wail.

"Now! now! Elspeth. You're all right. This is Hector McKay here with ye. We'll warn everybody about the Gauger, so don't you worry. Just you lie back and sleep, lass," said the old man, kindly. "Ben's here beside ye, Elspeth, so there's no need for ye to bother about a single thing." At that point Ben shot out a long pink tongue and licked Elspeth's face which seemed to reassure her, for she gave a flicker of a smile and settled down again.

Hearing Cleeve leading the pony from the stable, the Innkeeper hurried to the door. "Wait!" he cried. "I must ride down to Kirkhill myself. Elspeth has just managed to tell me that she had a message from the Minister – a warning of an excise raid. If you ride down with that kind of news they'll think it's a hoax. You bide here with Elspeth, and I'll ride the pony myself, if ye'll help me up into the saddle."

Cleeve had the decency to blush at the reminder of the mean trick he had tried to play on the Glen folk. "Is Elspeth conscious?" he enquired as he hoisted Mr McKay into the saddle.

"She was, but only for a wee while. I'll get a message to the doctor as soon as possible. See and look after her, and keep her warm, lad," and he spurred the pony up the hillside.

It was well after ten o'clock when the Innkeeper rode into his own backyard. As he dismounted, he noticed fresh hoof marks in the snow. Tethered in the shelter of the Innyard were two horses. "The Gauger's beat me!" was his first thought, but on looking closer, he recognised the horses as belonging to Tom McNeill and Geordie Farquharson. He heaved a sigh of relief and thumped loudly on the back door for admission. Mrs McKay had been listening for his return and appeared almost at once, with a lantern in her hand.

"Where have ye been all this time, Hector?" she cried. "I've been fair worried about ye, thinking ye'd got stuck in a snowdrift. Tom McNeill and Geordie Farquharson were just about to set out to look for ye."

"Well, I'm all right m'dear, as ye can see, but there's been some queer ongoings in the Glen this night, I can tell ye," he said wearily as he entered the Inn kitchen.

"What's happened, Hector?" inquired his two neighbours.

"Young Elspeth MacLaine's lying up in The Auld Biggin like Death itself. I rushed back to get a doctor. She's been shot in the arm, and there's another man been shot dead. Leo Cleeve's mixed up in it, some way or other. I left him up there with Elspeth, but I never asked him for an explanation. It didn't seem important to know the ins and outs of it all when further delay might cost Elspeth her life. Did the wife tell ye that Ben brought a flock of sheep into one of our fields? It was Ben that persuaded me to follow him to the Auld Biggin because his mistress was in need of help. He's really a wonderful beast. By the way, Anne, ye'll need to rouse young Henry and send him to Alyth for the Doctor."

"But the Doctor's up in Glenisla, Hector. He passed up this way heading for the Manse just after you left. Apparently the Minister's had an accident," explained his wife.

"Dear me! That means the Doctor'll likely bide up there till morning. We'll better send Henry to fetch him right away, for if I'm not mistaken it's a matter of life and death with Elspeth."

As his wife hurried from the room to fetch young Henry the

ostler, who slept in a loft above the stable, the Innkeeper turned urgently to the two men.

"The Gauger's on his way down the Glen, lads. Eslpeth managed to tell me. She said the Minister had sent her to warn us. I'll bet the cunning beggars were planning a moonlight raid, hoping to catch us off our guard in the midst of New Year celebrations. Will ye take word down the Glen? There's no time to lose."

"Aye, we'll see to that," said Tom McNeill, "but my, I'm worried about Elspeth. How on earth did she get as far as The Auld Biggin?"

"I doubt we'll just need to wait till she's able to tell us," replied the Innkeeper. "By the way, as soon as it's daylight I'd like ye both to have a look at those sheep Ben fetched in here."

"What we really came up to see ye about, Hector, was to discuss what was to be done about Sandy MacLaine," said Geordie Farquharson. "I'm sure he never stole anybody's sheep. We'll need to do something to help him out of this mess."

"Maybe these sheep'll throw some light on the subject," said the Innkeeper. "I sincerely hope so, for, like you, I couldn't believe such a thing of Sandy MacLaine. But you lads must away now with the news of the Gauger."

At this point young Henry dashed into the kitchen to get his boots which were drying at the fire, rubbing the sleep from his eyes as the Innkeeper's wife helped him into his jacket.

"What'll I tell the Doctor?" he inquired.

"Take him to The Auld Biggin straight away, Henry. Tell him it's urgent," answered Mr McKay. "Just take that pony I have at the door. It's fresh enough."

The other two men stayed only long enough to finish their drinks but, just as they emerged from the doorway of the Inn, a clatter of hoofs sounded in the yard and young Henry came galloping back.

"The Gauger's coming down the hill," he cried, as he reined in his horse.

"Maybe it's the Doctor coming back," suggested Tom McNeill.

"No, there was only the Doctor and his assistant when they went up past here," said Henry. "There's four or else five in this party. Some seem to be in uniform."

"Off ye go, lads, out the back way," said the Innkeeper. "I'll keep the Gauger and his mob here as long as I can. D'ye think they'd seen ye turning back, Henry?"

"Maybe they did. I couldn't be sure."

"Well never mind, away ye go and get the Doctor. That's the main thing." As Henry set off up the hill again, Mr McKay let the other two men out by another exit. "When ye call at The Shieling I wouldn't tell Mrs MacLaine about Elspeth in the meantime," he couselled. "She can do nothing and it would only worry her, but warn her about the Exciseman, of course, in case Sandy had some smuggling gear lying around. Mind and come back in the morning till we inspect the sheep."

When the two farmers reached The Shieling, Mrs MacLaine was still sitting up but she did not unbolt the door until she had made sure who the late callers were. Both men noticed how haggard she looked but neither broached the subject of the sheep stealing, although it was upper-most in their minds.

"The Exciseman's on one of his friendly visits," said Geordie Farquharson with an attempt at brightness. "We just cried in to warn ye."

"Thank you," said Mrs MacLaine. "I'll see that everything is out of sight. Can I give you a hot drink?"

"We just had a pint of ale at the Inn before we left," explained Tom McNeill. "Thanks all the same. I think we'd better keep going in case the Gauger's party don't stop at Kirkhill. We'll look in in the morning again."

"I've had no word from Sandy," said Mrs MacLaine sadly as she saw them out.

"Don't let yourself get downhearted now, Mary," said Geordie Farquharson, patting her shoulder. "It's a bad business, I grant ye, but nobody'll tell us that Sandy had a hand in any sheep stealing and I'm sure it'll all turn out all right yet, you'll see."

Those kindly words brought tears to Mrs MacLaine's eyes as she bade the men goodnight, but she felt cheered by the knowledge that she had such good neighbours.

When the Exciseman's party rode up to the Inn door the Landlord and his wife feigned surprise at such a late call but they opened their cellar and the rest of their premises for inspection. Afterwards they invited the company to join them in a glass of hot ale at the kitchen fire.

The crackling logs and the leaping flames were such a welcome sight on that cold frosty night that the men readily agreed. They seated themselves on the wooden settles and gratefully accepted the proffered drinks, even joining their hosts in singing "A Gude New Year Tae Ane and A" when the old grandfather clock in the corner chimed the midnight hour.

Then the old Innkeeper began to tell stories of bygone Hogmanays in the Glen, and a full hour elapsed before the Excisemen and the two troopers left to continue their journey. By that time the warning had been well and truly spread to all the homesteads in the Glen and no evidence of smuggling activities remained in view.

A Strange New Year's Morning

Young Henry found Glenisla still wide awake when he rode
over the footbridge and down past the Kirk to the Manse.
While crossing the hill he had heard the customary shots being
fired into the air at various outlying homesteads to mark the
passing of the Old Year. Now a group of merrymakers singing
"Should Auld Acquaintance be Forgot" strung themselves
out across the road and playfully tried to bar his way to the
Manse. They gathered round the pony crying "A Happy
New Year!" and each one insisted on shaking him by the
hand. Henry would have enjoyed a bit of fun with them, but
mindful of his master's urgency regarding the Doctor, he
begged them to let him pass. Tethering the pony to the
manse gate he hurried to the Minister's front door.

A light shone in an upstairs room and, as Henry banged

loudly on the door with his clenched fist, the window was pushed up and a head appeared.

"Hello there!" said a man's voice. "Mrs McAllister has gone to bed. Can I do anything to help you?"

"I'm from Kirkhill Inn, and I'm wanting the doctor," Henry called back.

"I'm the Doctor. What's the trouble?"

"There's been an accident at a croft away back in the hills there," explained Henry, waving a hand vaguely in the direction from which he had come. "There's a man dead and a lassie badly wounded. I've been sent to take you to the place, Doctor."

"Wait till I come down and let you in," said the Doctor, and he withdrew his head and closed the window.

But the Minister's housekeeper had also heard the knocking and the voices, and was already on her way, candle in hand, to unbolt the door.

"What's that you were saying, laddie, about a man being dead?" she queried, as soon as Henry had stepped inside.

"Aye, it's right enough, Mrs McAllister," said Henry, rather thrilled, if the truth be told, to be the bearer of such momentous news.

"What's his name, and which croft is it?"

"I wasn't told his name, but Ben, the MacLaine's dog, fetched some sheep down to Kirkhill about half nine o'clock and he led Mr McKay back over the hill to The Auld Biggin. Mr McKay found this man lying dead and Elspeth MacLaine wounded! I've to take the Doctor up there right away."

"Oh me! Oh my! This is terrible news!" exclaimed the housekeeper, wringing her hands. "The Minister'll be fair upset, that he will. Poor Elspeth! But she left here to go to Kirkhill with a message from the Minister. What could she be doing at The Auld Biggin? Nobody has lived there for the last twenty years."

At this point the Doctor and his assistant came downstairs and Mrs McAllister pulled herself together. "Will I make ye a dish of tea before ye go, Sirs?" she asked.

"Thank you, Mrs McAllister, it would certainly help to fortify us for the journey, and no doubt this young man will be glad of a reviver," the Doctor replied, indicating the Ostler. "Now, young man, tell me more about this accident, and where the place is."

So Henry once more related the tale as told by Mr McKay. While the Doctors were getting into their boots and capes, he re-told it to the Minister who had summoned Mrs McAllister and insisted that Henry be sent to his bedroom, where he now lay with his leg in splints, the Doctor having diagnosed a broken ankle bone.

In no time at all the travellers were ready, and Henry quickly saddled their horses and led them up the road and over the Isla on to the hill.

The young Ostler was none too sure of the exact location of the place, and as the house had been virtually uninhabited for so long, there was no track to follow. But the moon still shone brightly, and after about an hour, they saw the dark patch of buildings against the white landscape and spurred on their horses.

The dogs barked furiously as the horses drew near the ramshackle building, and Leo Cleeve opened the rickety door as the riders dismounted.

"Where is the girl?" the Doctor demanded, without preamble.

"In here," said Cleeve and stepped aside to let the men pass. He followed them to Elspeth's bedside while Henry remained outside with the horses.

Elspeth had recovered consciousness but appeared to be delirious, and lay tossing and turning on her bed of bracken, her eyes bright and restless. Ben lay beside her and seemed at first inclined to resent this intrusion, but Donald Matheson, the medical student, patted the collie's head and spoke kindly to him. So the faithful old dog decided to accept them as friends.

After a thorough examination of the patient's arm the Doctor turned to Donald Matheson.

"This is a very bad wound, as you can see, and this is certainly no place for an invalid. She must be removed from here as quickly as possible." Then, addressing Cleeve, he asked, "What did they say her name was, and where does she come from?"

"She's Elspeth MacLaine from The Shieling."

"Elspeth MacLaine! I thought somehow her face was familiar! My, how she's grown since I saw her last. She's quite the young lady now. What on earth was she doing up here? Was she alone?"

"I think she must have got lost in the mist," said Leo.

"Do you think it would be possible to get a cart up here?" asked the Doctor.

"Under present conditions I should say it would be quite impossible. There's no road or even a proper track to the place, but by daylight we could carry Elspeth down on a stretcher," suggested Leo.

"She must be got away from here, anyway. I fear pneumonia and that will mean a difficult struggle under favourable conditions. In this place there would be no hope at all. Where is my bag Donald? We must attend to this arm at once. Is the water in the kettle nearly boiling?" he demanded of Cleeve.

Divesting himself of cape and jacket the Doctor set to work, and for the next half hour both the medical student and Leo Cleeve were kept busy fetching and carrying and doing their best to soothe Elspeth until the wound in her arm had been properly cleaned and dressed. Then she was given a sleeping draught and only after he was quite satisfied that the medicine was having the desired effect did the Doctor ask to be taken to the dead man.

MacKeracher still lay where he had fallen, and after a quick examination, the Doctor ordered the body to be carried into a shed and covered up.

"Now," he said to Henry, "I want you to go back to Kirkhill and ask them to supply something which can be used as stretcher. Tell Mr McKay to send as many men up here as possible, for it'll be quite a journey and we'll need relays of stretcher bearers. In fact, Donald," he said, turning to his assistant, "I believe you'd better go with him. You will be able to see that we get everything we'll be likely to need. Have the girls parents been told what has happened, d'you know, Henry?"

"I don't think so," Henry replied.

"Well, Donald, you'd better break the news to them so that they can have a warm bed ready for the patient. I'll trust you to see to everything. And don't forget to get a message sent to the Town's Officers in Alyth about this fatal accident."

Having promised to attend to everything, Henry and Donald Matheson mounted and headed for Kirkhill.

It was now around three in the morning, and since the frost was very keen Cleeve and the Doctor returned to the house. While the Doctor went to look at his patient Cleeve built up the fire and got hot drinks for them both.

"You've some medical experience haven't you?" queried the Doctor as they thankfully sipped their drinks.

Unwilling to say much about himself, Cleeve hesitated.

"Why do you think that?" he asked guardedly.

"By the way you had attended to that wound. It was quite professional. And how do you happen to be in a place like this? You're English aren't you?"

Cleeve didn't answer at first. He continued to sip his drink and stare into the fire.

"I suppose my past is all likely to be dug up now, anyway," he said at last, "so I'll tell you the whole story if you care to listen."

"Go ahead," replied the Doctor. "We've got nothing better to do anyway."

Cleeve cleared his throat. "You were right about my having medical experience. I do know something about the profession for I attended classes as a medical student in Edinburgh for two sessions. I am English, but my mother was born in Edinburgh. That's why I came to study at that particular medical school. My father was always against my becoming a doctor. He wanted me to study law as he had done and his father before him. They wanted me to go into the family notary business. So my father refused to pay for my medical training. My mother had died before I left school and I had received a small legacy from her estate so I decided to use the money to train in medicine. I planned to eke out my living by working during vacations. Unfortunately, I got into bad company – like draws to like, or so 'tis said – and I soon got rid of my money. In the course of my somewhat riotous living I had come rather violently in contact with the excise officers in Leith, and one of the officers, at no small risk to himself, got me out of a tight corner. Soon after that, the Officer received a posting and we lost touch until I happened to come to this district looking for work at the harvest. We met again in Alyth and when the Exciseman heard where I was to be working he saw a way of getting his pound of flesh out of me. He told me this district was a hotbed of smuggling and asked me to keep a sharp lookout and report anything suspicious to him. When my harvest job was done he offered me work, and my first assignment was to return to the Glen and spy on the crofters. He had a clever plan worked out which I had to put into effect, but the Glen folk were too crafty and turned the tables on me. The Exciseman was furious and blamed me for the failure of his plan. He was still determined to get his pound of flesh out of me, though, so he didn't dismiss me as one might have expected. Of course I was angry too, about what had happened, and I was anxious for revenge on the Kilry crofters who had made such a fool of me.

"About this time I was introduced to an Angus MacKeracher – the man whose body lies out in the shed there – and after some slight acquaintance with me, he told me he was making a tidy sum out of sheep-stealing. Being none too large of cash, and having still a hankering to continue my medical studies, I was easily enticed into work which seemed to be proving so lucrative. I'm afraid I just didn't bother to think about the possible consequences of such a dishonest trade.

"This man MacKeracher seemed to be concentrating his activities mainly around the farms and crofts of Kilry. This suited me fine, the way I was feeling about those same crofters. MacKeracher seemed to have a special grudge against the MacLaines of The Shieling, though what it was I never learned and shall probably never know now. Anyway, just a night or two ago, we made a few well-planned raids and collected quite a flock up here intending to take them over the hills by moonlight. This was actually my first job with him, so I must be the unlucky one. We were waiting for the mist to clear and somehow or other Elspeth there had stumbled across our hide-out. My guess is that she had recognised her pet lamb amongst the flock and had realised that the sheep had been stolen. Whatever way it was, she took the sheep out of the fank and was heading over the hill with them when we discovered what was happening. We had no idea who had taken the sheep of course. Angus MacKeracher ran for his gun and fired some shots one of which hit Elspeth. As he was running forward to get another shot, he tripped and his gun went off, killing him instantly.

"There was another man with us – a brother, or half-brother, of MacKeracher's. I'd had an instinctive dislike of this man from the moment I first met him and my instincts proved correct for I now know him to be a proper rat. He cleared off after the tragedy, but I'd had a sickening feeling that the person who'd taken the sheep might be Elspeth and I felt sure she'd been wounded. I decided I must go and look for her. If I hadn't found her I daresay I'd have cleared off too. Now, I suppose, I'll have to pay the price."

"You've certainly got yourself into a sorry mess," said the Doctor, "but in my opinion, you'll be better to make a clean breast of the whole thing – just as you've done to me. It's your only hope as far as I can see. As an accomplice in such a serious crime I believe you may be severely dealt with, but I hardly think you'll be doomed to pay the supreme penalty."

As the hours passed, the Doctor gave Elspeth constant

care and attention. Cleeve kept the fire blazing so that the temperature of the room wouldn't fall. "Thank goodness MacKeracher had a good store of fuel built up here," he said.

Every now and then one or other would go to the door to view the weather conditions.

"I'm afraid there's more snow coming," said the Doctor, "and if we're trapped up here, that child's life's as good as lost."

Gradually conversation flagged and the only sounds were the crackling of the logs on the fire and the moaning of the wind round the dilapidated building. Daybreak was just beginning to lighten the sky when the sound of hoofs padding over the snow came to their ears.

"What's that?" exclaimed the Doctor, tilting his head to listen.

"It can't be the rescue party," said Cleeve. "I should think they'd only be leaving Kirkhill about now. They'd never attempt the journey in the dark and the moon's been obscured for some time now. It might be someone come on ahead though. I'll go and see."

He was back in a few minutes, his face more ashen than before.

"It's Mac's horse, and it's riderless!" he gasped.

"Mac? D'you mean that scoundrel who cleared out and left you?"

"Yes. He must've been thrown."

"We certainly can't go and look for him, that's for sure," said the Doctor. "When Donald Matheson comes back he'll maybe go with you though. I sincerely hope that blackguard is brought in alive to take his share of the consequences of this night's work."

Cleeve led the horse round to the stable where the prize rams belonging to Tom McNeill and Geordie Farquharson lay beside the other horses, ruminating contentedly.

It was one of those dark, dreary, winter mornings when the sigh of the wind gives warning of an approaching snowstorm and the white capped hills stand out bleakly against the leaden grey of the sky. Cleeve shuddered as he crossed to the house to rejoin the Doctor.

"How is she now?" he inquired, nodding towards Elspeth.

"Not much change either way, as far as I can see."

They lapsed into silence once more. Then, at last there came the welcome sound of approaching voices.

"Thank the Lord!" exclaimed the Doctor, with a sigh of relief. "I'll be glad to get away from this place, I can tell you. This has been the strangest New Year's morning I've ever experienced in my whole life."

All Hands to the Rescue

When Henry the Ostler and Donald Matheson, the student,
arrived back at Kirkhill Inn, just after four in the morning,
they found both the Innkeeper and his wife astir, for neither
had felt like going to bed after the Excisemen had left. They
had just snatched what sleep they could get sitting by the fire.
The sound of the horses sent both of them hurrying to the
door, and the men had hardly alighted when the old people
were plying them with questions about Elspeth.

Donald explained the Doctor's instructions regarding
stretchers and blankets and also told them that he must
go to Elspeth's home to break the news to her parents.
So they, in turn, explained to him the dreadful misfortune
that had befallen Elspeth's father, and advised him not to
tell Mrs MacLaine the whole story of Elspeth's accident,

in case another shock should prove rather much for the poor woman.

"Thank you for telling me," said Donald. "I shall try not to upset Mrs MacLaine more than is absolutely necessary."

"Come away and get something to eat now lads, for ye must both be in need of sustenance," said the hospitable old landlord, and the two young men did justice to the hearty meal set before them.

"I'm sure I have two doors that would do for stretchers, and we've plenty of blankets. I'll get out a sledge and we'll have everything ready for ye when ye come back from The Shieling," said Mr McKay. "The McNeill laddies and the young Farquharsons will doubtless lend a hand if ye ask them."

"The Town's Officers in Alyth will have to be notified regarding the man's death too," Donald said.

"Aye, we'll see to that as well. I think, maybe, there'll be more than that message for the Town's Officers."

So Donald rode down to see Mrs MacLaine, while Henry continued to Kilwhin where he roused the McNeill family. All the men, including Rory, hastily donned boots and cloaks and set out for Kirkhill as soon as they had fed their animals. Lachlan also made a detour to Drumedge to give the Farquharsons the news.

By first light the rescue party were gathered in the yard at Kirkhill. There were seven of them: Rab and Lachlan McNeill and Rory, Dave and Jock Farquharson, Donald Matheson and Henry. Having loaded the stretchers and the blankets on to the sledge, they set out at once.

After they had gone, Mr McNeill, Mr Farquharson, and Mr McKay rounded up the sheep that Ben had fetched into the field the night before and it didn't take those keen-eyed sheep farmers long to identify sheep from their own flocks even though the marks of ownership had been carefully obliterated. Since Mr McKay had told the other two about Daisy following Ben over the hill, they were quite sure the remaining sheep would belong to The Shieling.

"This'll clear Sandy MacLaine, thank goodness," said Tom McNeill, "but we'd better not let Leo Cleeve slip through our fingers until we have the full story. I'll ride down to Alyth right away and fetch the Town's Officers."

"I'll need to get back to Drumedge and get the cattle fed," said Geordie Farquharson, "but I'll come back later and see what's what." So the two men rode over the moor together and Tom McNeill proceeded to Alyth where he sought an interview with the Senior Town Officer. Having explained the happenings of the night, and the recovery of the stolen sheep, Tom McNeill requested that Sandy MacLaine be released.

"We are detaining him until Thursday, when he is to be formally charged with the crime of sheep stealing," the Officer explained, "but I must admit I was loathe to arrest him. Having known him over the past year or two, it was difficult to believe him capable of a mean theft. Unfortunately, the evidence was strong against him."

"Well, the evidence is now strongly in his favour," Tom McNeill pointed out, "for, as I've just told you, we've got the sheep, and one of the thieves, and another has been shot dead up at The Auld Biggin croft. The Doctor wants you to go up and investigate the death, so why not bring Sandy MacLaine up with you?"

"This is not just a trick to get MacLaine out of jail, is it?" demanded the Officer.

"It is not, Sir, on my honour as a gentleman."

"You have definite, concrete proof of this man's innocence?"

"We have indeed. All that you, or anybody else could require."

The Officer thought the matter over for a few minutes. At last he made up his mind. "All right," he said, "I'll let MacLaine accompany us up the Glen on condition that he returns here should I consider myself dissatisfied with the proof offered."

"That seems fair enough, Sir," Tom McNeill agreed, so

the Officer ordered the prisoner to be brought in, that he might have the matter put before him.

Naturally, Sandy MacLaine was only too willing to agree to the Officer's proposal, and was absolutely overjoyed at this turn of events.

Tom McNeill stepped forward with both hands extended, to welcome his neighbour. "Oh my, Sandy!" he cried, "I can't tell ye how glad I am to see ye, nor how sorry we've all been that ye should have to suffer this terrible injustice. But it's all right now, man. I'm sure of that."

"I must admit, things did look black for me, Tom," said Sandy MacLaine. "What with all the lies those chaps at the Blackthorn managed to tell, and the fact that I was definitely at the Inn on the night in question, I'm not surprised I was arrested. However, I'll soon get over it, if I was just back home again with Mary and Elspeth."

As they journeyed up the Glen, Tom McNeill told Sandy what he knew about Elspeth's part in the happenings of the previous night. As he listened, Sandy's happiness at being released quickly turned into a sickening fear for his daughter's life.

On reaching The Shieling they found Mrs MacLaine attending to the household chores. She was quite overcome at the sight of her husband, and clung to him in tears, but the men could not delay long.

"I'm sorry I can't leave your husband with you just yet, Mrs MacLaine," said the Senior Officer." We must get this matter properly investigated first, but from what Mr McNeill has told us, I think you can be quite sure that your husband will be exonerated."

The rescue party, in the meantime, had made good progress. When they arrived at The Auld Biggin, Elspeth was quite conscious, and on hearing Rory's voice, she asked to see him, but the Doctor would only allow them a few words together. Ben was delighted to see Rory and even left his vigil by Elspeth's bedside to follow Rory to the door, where Daisy also promptly made her presence known.

Wrapped in blankets, Elspeth was made as comfortable as possible on the improvised stretcher and the men worked in relays as planned. Rory walked at one side and the Doctor on the other, while Ben and Daisy brought up the rear of the stretcher party. One of the young men lead the dead man's horse, with the corpse strapped over the saddle. Cleeve had shown the boys their father's rams and they had decided they'd better take them back right away, also Angus MacKeracher's dogs, in case of a storm developing. So it was quite a cavalcade that made the journey over the hills from the ruined croft.

Snow was beginning to fall when they set out, and by the time they sighted Kirkhill it was blowing quite a blizzard so it was decided the patient would be taken no farther that night.

The Innkeeper's wife, fortunately, had anticipated this and had already prepared the box-bed in the Inn-parlour, so Elspeth was tucked up there, much to her disappointment. She was full of anxiety about her father, and anxious, also, to be re-united with her mother, so she was inclined to be fretful.

"Don't worry, Elspeth," said Rory, "as soon as I've had something to eat I'll go down for your Mother. You lie down and sleep. Then you'll be ready to tell her all the tale when you see her."

Back at the old croft, as soon as the stretcher party had left, Leo Cleeve and Donald Matheson had got out their ponies, and the one belonging to the missing man, and set off to look for him.

At first they found the track easy to follow, but tracking became more difficult as the snow continued. They had covered a considerable distance before they began to see signs of any mishap. As far as they could make out, the rider had been thrown when the horse had stumbled into a hill burn which was concealed under great wreaths of snow. In falling, the man had become entangled in the reins, and so had been dragged along, over rocks, and through bogs and burns until finally they found him almost buried in a snow-drift. Here, it became obvious that the horse had become bogged down altogether. In an effort to free itself, it had flailed around with all four feet, giving its master a severe beating-up in the process. Eventually, it had floundered free and, in so doing, had cast off its human burden and returned riderless to the old croft.

Donald Matheson examined the man where he lay.

"He's still alive," he said, "but I think he's lucky to be that, for he's badly smashed up. To begin with, he has a broken nose, and I shouldn't be surprised if his jaw is badly damaged too, for he has certainly had a few teeth knocked out. One eye is almost out of sight and his right cheek bone is smashed. I guess the horse must have kicked him in the face several times." He felt the injured man's shoulder and frowned. "His collar bone seems to be broken, and I'm sure there's some fractured ribs. Probably internal injuries and maybe even brain damage. I can't attempt to patch him up right here in this blizzard. All we can do is tie him across the saddle of his horse and get him back to the old croft, if not to the Inn."

The blizzard had abated somewhat by the time they had retraced their steps to the Auld Biggin, and both men decided that the best plan would be to proceed to Kirkhill without further delay.

On their arrival at Kirkhill the Doctor and Donald set to work without delay to bring life back into the stiff, frozen body of the sheep stealer, and by the application of artificial respiration, and the administering of quantities of brandy, he did eventually regain consciousness. While they were attending to his multiple injuries he opened his eyes and uttered a volley of oaths.

"I think he'll pull through," said the Doctor. "We'll leave him for a bit."

"My, you lads have had a hard night of it, Doctor," remarked the old Innkeeper.

"Donald has been a lot harder put to it than I have though," answered the Doctor. "He'll need to sleep the clock round when he gets back to Alyth."

"Do you still feel the medical profession is what you want?" he asked, turning with a grin towards his young assistant.

"Oh, yes! More than ever now, Sir," replied Donald. "I'll admit, I am tired, but all this has been very exciting. I'd no idea when I decided to answer your advertisement for assistance that so much could happen around an isolated little place like Alyth."

As the Doctor and Donald drew in chairs beside the others at the Innkeeper's hospitable table, the Doctor inquired of Cleeve who exactly the injured man was.

"His name is Adam MacKeracher. That's about all I know, except that he recently became landlord of the Blackthorn Inn. He and the dead man were brothers – or maybe it was half-brothers. There wasn't much resemblance, as far as I could see."

"He's a pretty tough character whoever he is," observed the Doctor.

At this point, Rory, who had been about to set out for The Shieling, called from the doorway, "There's four men coming up the road on horseback! It's Father and the Town's Officers, and they have Mr MacLaine with them!"

The Mystery is Solved

When Rory announced that the horsemen were approaching,
the men pushed back their chairs and went outside in time to
see the party from Alyth ride into the yard.

While Sandy MacLaine's neighbours hurried forward to
greet him, the Senior Officer dismounted and handed his
reins to Henry.

"Where is the dead man?" he asked without preliminary.

"He's in the stable," replied the Innkeeper, crossing to
open the stable door. The Doctor and Leo Cleeve followed
the Officers inside, both knowing they would be required to
answer questions. The other men grouped themselves around
the doorway.

First of all the Officer bent and examined the body, while
the Doctor gave his report on the cause of death, and Leo

Cleeve described exactly how the accident had occurred. Then the Officer removed the man's private possessions from his pockets and saddle bag.

"His name was Ralph McIntyre. Is that right?" he inquired, studying the document he had just found amongst the man's belongings, but before Cleeve could reply, Sandy MacLaine pushed his way forward.

"Ralph McIntyre!" he exclaimed. "Did you say Ralph McIntyre?"

"That's the name written here," the Officer assured him.

"That was the name of the scoundrel my late sister was married to, but we haven't heard of him for about twenty years. Surely this man isn't Ralph McIntyre!"

"What was your sister's name?" asked the Officer. "He appears to have all his worldly possessions with him, for this is a marriage certificate, I think. Unfortunately, it is scarcely readable."

"My sister's name was Isabella Anna MacLaine."

"Yes. That's the name written here. It's almost obliterated, but I can just make that out. See for yourself." He handed the faded document to Sandy MacLaine.

"I never actually met the man, but I have seen a picture of him so I might remember his face," said Mr MacLaine, and he bent down to look at the dead man.

"But this is Angus MacKeracher!" he exclaimed, obviously astounded.

At this point Leo Cleeve interrupted. "We all knew him as Angus MacKeracher, but that's not to say his real name wasn't Ralph McIntyre."

Mr MacLaine turned back to look at the dead man again. He was visibly moved, and indeed it was not surprising for the face he looked upon was the face of the man who had rescued Elspeth from the river on the day of the sheep sale. He recalled how, on that occasion, he had experienced a feeling of familiarity and now the explanation was apparent, for this was also the face of the young man on the wedding picture. The face was older of course, and now somewhat camouflaged by a thick beard, but it was definitely the same face.

"Aye, it's him all right," he said at last, turning away. "Many's the time I wished I could meet that man face to face, and my wish was granted, though I didn't realise it at the time, unfortunately – and now it's too late. He vowed vengeance on the MacLaines when my father turned him out of the house, and by jove, he nearly had vengeance on me! To think I might have gone to the gallows for his crime!"

At this juncture Leo Cleeve interrupted again. "I often wondered why he had such a grudge against the name MacLaine, but that explains it."

"By heavens! and it's clear to me now too!" cried Tom McNeill, striking his fist on the stable door. "That blackguard was a clever rogue, if ever there was one! He stole sheep from our places and passed by The Shieling deliberately so that suspicion would fall on you, Sandy. When he took your sheep from Kirkhill he thought they were the property of the Inn-keeper. He certainly meant to ruin the good name of the MacLaines."

"But what I can't understand is why the new Innkeeper of the Blackthorn could want to tell so many lies about me," said Mr MacLaine, quite bewildered by all this. "He couldn't have had anything against me, for I never even heard of the man before he came to the Alyth district, and it was his false testimony against me that landed me in jail you must remember."

"That's easily explained," said Cleeve, "for the new land-lord of the Blackthorn was hand-in-glove with this man. In fact, they posed as brothers, both going under the name MacKeracher, and the Innkeeper was in on the sheep stealing too. He's the injured man that's lying in the Kirkhill kitchen right now."

"So that's it!" exclaimed Mr MacLaine. "They were in league against me! The call I got to go to the Blackthorn last Friday had been a well-planned hoax! And of course," he added, bitterly, "I fell headlong into the trap!"

"Tell me, how did you come to be associated with this man McIntyre alias MacKeracher," the Officer enquired, turning to Cleeve.

"Well, it's a long story, and one I'm heartily ashamed of," replied Cleeve, and he repeated what he had already told the Doctor during their vigil by Elspeth's bedside in the old ruined croft.

Like the Doctor, the Officer was of the opinion that Cleeve had been more of a fool than anything else to become implicated with these criminals. "But that won't absolve you from blame," he remarked, "and I must place you under arrest. Now, where is this other man you speak of?" Leo Cleeve led the way from the stable to the Inn, followed by the others.

The injured man was now showing signs of regaining consciousness, but was as yet unable to speak.

"In pretty bad shape, is he?" the Officer inquired of the Doctor.

"Well, he has taken quite a hammering," and the Doctor explained the accident as Cleeve and Matheson had believed it to have happened, "but I think he'll pull through, nevertheless. His kind always do."

"What about Elspeth, Doctor?" Sandy MacLaine now asked. "Can I see her?"

"Oh yes, there's the little girl too," interrupted the Officer. "I'd forgotten about her part in all this sordid business. We'll need a statement from her, for I understand she has been the means of everything being brought to light."

"I'm afraid the child is not in a fit state to be questioned, meantime," said the Doctor. "She is suffering severely from shock."

"Excuse me, Doctor," Mrs McKay broke in at this point, "I'd like you to have a look at Elspeth. She seems very restless, and is continually asking for her father and mother."

The Doctor hurried off to see his patient.

"You may go in and see her," he said to Sandy MacLaine when he came back, "but don't stay long, and don't let her get excited, whatever you do."

"Hello, Elspeth!" said her father as he approached the bed, and Elspeth turned a flushed face towards him.

"Oh Father, I'm so glad to see you!" she cried. "I thought you were in jail."

"So I was, Elspeth, but thanks to you and Ben, I'm a free man again."

"Ben took the sheep to Kirkhill then?" Elspeth queried, and as her father assured her of the dog's safe delivery of the flock, her eyes filled with tears.

"Dear Ben! He had to do it all by himself, Father. I just couldn't go any further. Where is Ben now?"

"He's here at the fireside, waiting for you." The collie thumped his tail as his master bent to pat his head.

"Wasn't it lucky I found Daisy too?" said Elspeth.

"It was indeed," agreed her father.

"I was hurrying to Kirkhill with a message from the Minister about the Exciseman, and I got lost in the mist you know," and Elspeth went on the relate as much as she could recall of the happenings of the night before.

"Well, you got the message through in time, Elspeth, and all was well. Now you'd better get some rest, or the Doctor will be raging at me. Rory has gone down for your mother, and they'll be here any minute."

So, greatly relieved at the knowledge that her father was safe, Elspeth slept again, unaware of the drama that was unfolding around her.

By this time the injured Adam MacKeracher had recovered sufficiently to look around him, and at sight of the uniformed Town's Officers he received an unwelcome shock. Anxious to avoid taking any blame for the sheep stealing he cried out, "Don't blame me. I didn't steal the sheep. I would never have been there if it hadn't been for all the lies he told me."

"Is that so? But tell me this, why did you tell so many lies about this innocent man?" demanded the Officer, indicating Mr MacLaine.

"I was forced to do it."

"By whom?"

"McIntyre."

"But we were lead to believe that the dead man's name was MacKeracher. He was your brother, was he not?

"No, no. He wasn't my brother. His name was Ralph McIntyre. He took the name MacKeracher so that folk up around here wouldn't identify him. He had been married to a MacLaine and he hated all the MacLaines. I was living in peace on my croft near Burrelton until he got me involved in all this. It was him that got me into the Blackthorn Inn. He planned everything," whined MacKeracher.

"Well, he can't answer for his sins now, but you can certainly answer for yours," said the Officer, "and I place you under arrest."

The snow having now abated somewhat, it was decided to borrow a cart to take the dead man and the two prisoners to Alyth.

Just as they were preparing to leave, Mrs MacLaine and Rory arrived.

"How is Elspeth?" Mrs MacLaine enquired anxiously of the Doctor.

"She is not out of the wood by any means," he replied, "but I'm sure of one thing. She'll be much happier now that you are here, and I'm glad you're here too, for I'll be able to leave you in charge while I return to Alyth. Tomorrow I shall come back and bring the medicines she requires, and fresh bandages for her arm. I am leaving sufficient medicines to be administered during the night and the instructions are written on the labels, so you shouldn't have any difficulty."

The injured MacKeracher was now made as comfortable as possible in the cart, and despite many objections on his part, the corpse was placed beside him. Cleeve was instructed to take the reins, and the two Officers took up their positions on either side of the cart and the cavalcade moved off. The Doctor and Donald Matheson followed very soon after, all being anxious to reach the town before darkness fell.

Mrs MacLaine and Rory found Elspeth in a very restless,

feverish condition. She seemed to be worrying about her grandparents and could talk of nothing else.

"The Minister's housekeeper said she would go to Granny, but the Minister will be needing all her attention after his accident. Granny will be wondering where I am. I must go to her," and she kept tossing aside the bedclothes.

"You're not fit to get out of bed, Elspeth," said her mother, "and there's no need to worry about the old people. Mrs McAllister is a very capable person, and she will attend to them as she said she would, I'm sure of that. You just settle down and try to get some rest, and your father will ride up the Glen tomorrow and see how everything is."

"If Mr MacLaine can't manage I'll go, Elspeth," said the ever-obliging Rory. So between them, they succeeded in pacifying her. But both were worried, for it was obvious she was running a very high fever and her condition was deteriorating.

The Sassenach no More

The Doctor's worst fears were realised, and Elspeth did develop pneumonia and became very ill indeed. Several times her life was despaired of, but her strong constitution stood her in good stead and she pulled through. Unfortunately, the wound in her arm became infected, and for a time it was feared that the arm would need to be amputated. Thanks to the skill and care of the Doctor and his assistant, however, that catastrophe was also averted.

It was six weeks before Elspeth could be moved from Kirkhill and it was nearly three months before she was able to be out and about. Even then the Doctor said she was not to be allowed back to school until the weather was warmer.

"Let her get out on the moor and breathe the pure

mountain air into her lungs. That will do her more good than lessons in the meantime," he advised.

As soon as she felt better, Elspeth began to take an interest in everything again and asked eagerly how things were going at the bothy.

"I have decided to give up the smuggling altogether, Elspeth," her father replied. "After all that has happened I think I've learned my lesson."

Mrs MacLaine and the Minister were delighted to hear this piece of news, but Elspeth wasn't so sure.

"I'm sorry Father has decided to give up the smuggling," she confided to Rory. "I thought it was exciting. Didn't you? I really enjoyed it."

"Aye. But it was just fun to us. We weren't running the risks that the men were," Rory pointed out. "My father and Mr Farquharson have decided to give it up as well."

"So that will be the end of the 'still' altogether then," said Elspeth with a sigh. "Oh well, I suppose everything has to come to an end sometime, but I'm glad I took part in the smuggling, Rory. When I grow old I'll be able to tell my grandchildren about the really exciting events in the Glen – tales that will be handed down from generation to generation."

The trial of Adam MacKeracher and Leo Cleeve took place in April, and Sandy MacLaine and his neighbours were required to give evidence for the prosecution. Elspeth was also cited as a witness but the Doctor was adamant that her health was in no fit state for the journey to Perth, so the Town's Officers came again to The Shieling and she gave a detailed statement regarding the fateful Hogmanay.

"How did it go, Father?" Elspeth enquired anxiously, on her father's return from the trial.

"Well, Adam MacKeracher was unanimously found guilty of acting as an accomplice in the crime of sheep stealing. He was condemned to deportation to Botany Bay for life. He'll never be back here again. Cleeve was convicted of involvement to a minor degree only, and was ordered to serve five years in the Forces overseas."

"I wish they'd pardoned Leo Cleeve," said Elspeth. "After all, he saved my life. Did they read out what I said about his staying behind to look for me, and then attending to my wound, when he could easily have got away?"

"Yes, they did read out your statement, Elspeth, and what you said weighed strongly in Leo's favour. Also the Doctor spoke well on his behalf. Otherwise I have no doubt he'd have got a much heavier sentence. Sheep stealing is a very serious crime, you must remember."

The Doctor had told Elspeth Cleeve's life story as told to him that night in The Auld Biggin. After the trial he was able to tell her that Cleeve had declared his intention of returning to the study of medicine as soon as he was released from the army.

"I think that young man has the makings of a good doctor, Elspeth," he said.

When the day came for Elspeth's return to school she felt very nervous indeed. She dreaded the resurrection of her hated nickname and was glad of Rory by her side as she approached the school. But a wonderful surprise was in store.

The Dominie, who had not been entirely unaware of what had been going on amongst his pupils in the months before Elspeth's illness, had had a word with Rory. From him he had learned how much Elspeth had suffered from the nickname and he decided to do something about it. So he made sure that everyone in the school understood just what Elspeth's pluck and loyalty had meant to her father and indeed to all her neighbours in the Glen.

When Elspeth entered the classroom the Dominie stepped forward with hand outstretched. "Welcome back, Elspeth," he said. "We are all proud to have you here amongst us. Three cheers for Elspeth MacLaine!"

And her schoolfellows practically raised the roof so heartily did they respond. It was a wonderful thrill for Elspeth. She was the Sassenach no more!

Sometime later, as Elspeth lay amongst the bracken in her

usual haunt beside the burn, with her father's two cows grazing nearby and Ben scratching for rabbits in a sandy bank, she thought of all that had happened to her and heaved a sigh of contentment.

"Thank goodness it's all past," she said to herself.

Just then Rory's familiar call sounded from out on the moor. Elspeth sat up and watched with interest as two black-and-white collies came bounding down the slope ahead of Rory and dashed over to join Ben's rabbit hunt.

"I'm so glad you took the dogs, Rory," Elspeth greeted him.

"So am I," agreed Rory. "They're great dogs! Some folk said we'd need to destroy them 'cos they'd never work for anybody else. Well, they certainly wouldn't work for my father or my brothers but I've had no bother with them. Here, Mac! Here, Kercher!" he called, and the dogs came at once, looking up at their new master with obvious affection.

"Mac and Kercher! Very apt, Rory," said Elspeth. "How did you think of it?"

"Och well," said Rory, "maybe MacKeracher wasn't all he should have been, but he was a marvellous dog-trainer and I thought he should be remembered for that."

"Here! Here! but actually his name wasn't MacKeracher. It was Ralph McIntyre. He was my uncle."

"I know that, but he'll always be MacKeracher to everybody here. I'm determined I'll make his dogs the best dogs in the whole of Scotland," said Rory quite seriously. "I used to think there couldn't be a better dog than Ben after what he did for you on Hogmanay, but Mac and Kercher are good dogs too, Elspeth."

"There'll never be a better dog than Ben as far as I'm concerned," said Elspeth, stooping to hug Ben who had just joined the group. "But of course he's growing old, and your dogs are quite young, Rory. I wish you every success with them. I hope they'll turn out well. I really do. By the way, has Blind Betsy been back in the Glen?"

"No. Blind Betsy's dead," Rory replied.

"How d'you know?"

"Because we had her son and his wife round in the Spring. They told us. But what on earth put Blind Betsy into your head at this very moment?" Rory asked, turning to stare at Elspeth in surprise.

Elspeth grinned. "Just before you joined me, I was thinking over all that had happened to me. And, d'you know, Rory, Blind Betsy warned me it was going to happen, only I didn't really believe her. She asked me never to tell anyone what she had read in my hand as long as she lived. You see she said there were people who thought she was a witch and that she should be burned at the stake. I promised I wouldn't tell, and I kept my promise, but now that she's gone, no one can ever harm her, so I'll tell you what she said to me.

"To begin with, I remember, she told me that my life would be fraught with many dangers, and before the heather bloomed twice on the hill there would be both flood an fire. Well there was the flood on the day of the sheep sale and I was very nearly drowned. Then there was the fire at the bothy and, as you know, I had a lucky escape there too. After that, Blind Betsy went on to tell me that three dark strangers would cross my path. She said that one whom I thought to be a friend might prove to be an enemy, and one that I took to be an enemy might yet prove to be a friend."

Rory laughed. "It all sounds a bit of a conundrum to me, Elspeth."

"Yes, it did to me too at the time, but I can understand it now. Angus MacKeracher was the one I imagined to be my friend."

"Because he rescued you from the river?"

"Yes I suppose so, and I always thought Leo Cleeve was an enemy but it all turned out in reverse, as you now know. About the third dark stranger, Betsy said she could tell me nothing except that he would cast a very dark shadow across my path because there was much evil in him."

"That would be Adam MacKeracher,' said Rory. "He certainly was a nasty piece of work."

"Yes, you're right. It was Adam MacKeracher. Then, after all that about the dark strangers, Betsy began to ramble a bit. She seemed to have forgotten I was there and I felt sure she was re-living events in her own life – those terrible things you told me that happened to her after Culloden. She was muttering away about the sound of gunfire and the Shadow of Death and the shadow of the gallows – things I felt sure could never come into my life. But you see, Rory, Betsy actually could look into the future. It was definitely my fortune she was telling, and it all happened to me in the space of one year, just as she said it would. In fact, every bit of Blind Betsy's prophecy came true!"

CATCH A KELPIE

If you enjoyed this book
you would probably enjoy our other Kelpies.

Here's a complete list to choose from:

for further details of Canongate Kelpies write to
Canongate Publishing, 17 Jeffrey Street, Edinburgh